"Mo? You'd better come over here."

She turned to find Brick next to a large pine tree on the mountainside's edge. As she approached, she saw the crude heart carved into the pine's bark.

There were two sets of initials at the center: her sister Tricia's, a plus sign and JP. Tricia's secret lover had used her maiden name initial. Wishful thinking on his part? Or is that the last name she'd given him?

"Know anyone with those initials?" Brick asked.

Mo shook her head. "I have no idea who JP is."

A gunshot echoed through the trees, splintering the bark on the tree next to her. Several nearby birds took flight, wings flapping wildly as Brick lunged for Mo, taking them both to the ground.

The second shot ricocheted off the tree where they had been standing, sending bark flying. And then there was nothing but the sound of the breeze in the pines and the seemingly hushed roar of the creek. Not even the birds sang...

DOUBLE ACTION DEPUTY

New York Times Bestselling Author

B.J. DANIELS

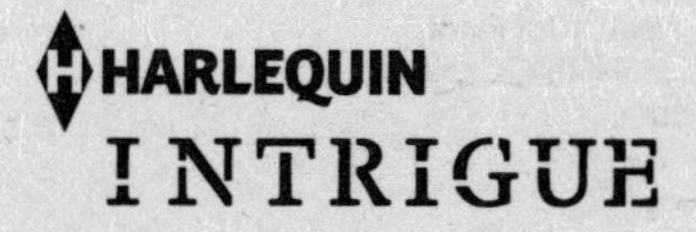

This book is for Kay Hould for all her loving support and encouragement. She is definitely not the gray-haired historical society woman in my Whitehorse, Montana series. But that is how we first met because of it.

ISBN-13: 978-1-335-13657-2

Double Action Deputy

This edition published by arrangement with Harlequin Books S.A.

For questions and comments about the quality of this book, please contact us at CustomerService@Harlequin.com.

Harlequin Enterprises ULC
22 Adelaide St. West, 40th Floor
Toronto, Ontario M5H 4E3, Canada
www.Harlequin.com

Printed in U.S.A.

B.J. Daniels is a *New York Times* and *USA TODAY* bestselling author. She wrote her first book after a career as an award-winning newspaper journalist and author of thirty-seven published short stories. She lives in Montana with her husband, Parker, and three springer spaniels. When not writing, she quilts, boats and plays tennis. Contact her at bjdaniels.com, on Facebook or on Twitter, @bjdanielsauthor.

Books by B.J. Daniels

Harlequin Intrigue

Cardwell Ranch: Montana Legacy

Steel Resolve
Iron Will
Ambush Before Sunrise
Double Action Deputy

Whitehorse, Montana: The Clementine Sisters

Hard Rustler
Rogue Gunslinger
Rugged Defender

The Montana Cahills

Cowboy's Redemption

Whitehorse, Montana: The McGraw Kidnapping

Dark Horse
Dead Ringer
Rough Rider

HQN Books

Montana Justice

Restless Hearts
Heartbreaker

Sterling's Montana

Stroke of Luck
Luck of the Draw
Just His Luck

The Montana Cahills

Renegade's Pride
Outlaw's Honor
Hero's Return
Rancher's Dream

Visit the Author Profile page at Harlequin.com.

CAST OF CHARACTERS

Brick Savage—The deputy marshal feared he wasn't up to the job—until he busted the suspended homicide cop out of jail.

Maureen "Mo" Mortensen—The suspended homicide cop was determined to get justice. Even if it meant taking a green deputy marshal with her.

Natalie Berkshire—The nanny-nurse was a woman with a lot of secrets. But even the guilty aren't guilty of everything they're accused of sometimes.

Marshal Hud Savage—He was worried his son had no idea what he was getting himself into and it could get him killed.

Dana Cardwell Savage—The last thing she wanted was for her son to follow in his father's footsteps. But she was a woman who had faith and knew when to let go.

Thomas Colton—He'd lost more than the woman he loved and his newborn son.

Tricia Colton—Mo's sister had the biggest secret of them all and she'd taken it to the grave with her.

Chapter One

Ghostlike, the woman stumbled out of the dark night and into the glare of his headlights. The tattered bedsheet wrapped around her fluttered in the breeze along with the duct tape that dangled from her wrists and one ankle.

He saw her look up as if she hadn't heard his pickup bearing down on her until the last moment. The night breeze lifted wisps of her dark hair from an ashen face as she turned her vacant gaze on him an instant before he slammed on his brakes.

The air filled with the smell and squeal of tires burning on the dark pavement as the pickup came to a shuddering halt. He sat for a moment, gripping the wheel and staring in horror into the glow of his headlights and seeing…nothing. Nothing but the empty street ahead just blocks from his apartment.

He threw the truck into Park and jumped out, convinced, even though he hadn't felt or heard a thud, that he'd hit her and that he'd find her lying bleeding on the pavement. How could he have missed her?

If there'd been a woman at all.

In those few seconds, leaving the driver's side door gaping open, the engine running, he was terrified of what he would find—and even more terrified of what he wouldn't.

Could he have just imagined the woman in his headlights? It wouldn't be the first time he'd had a waking nightmare since he'd come home to recuperate. He felt the cold breeze in his face even though it was June in Montana. The temperature at night dropped this time of year, the mountains still snowcapped. He shivered as he rounded the front of the truck and stopped dead.

His heart dropped to his boots.

The pavement was empty.

His pulse thundered in his ears.

I am losing my mind. I hallucinated the woman.

For months, he'd assured himself he was fine. Except for the nightmares that plagued him, something he'd done his best to keep from his family since returning to Cardwell Ranch.

Doubt sent a stab of alarm through him that made him weak with worry. He leaned against the front of the pickup. Why would he imagine such an image? What was wrong with him? He'd *seen* her. He'd seen every detail.

He really *was* losing his mind.

As he glanced around the empty street, he suddenly felt frighteningly all alone as if he was the last person left alive on the earth. This late at night, the new businesses were dark in this neighborhood, some still under construction. The ones that were opened closed early, making the area a ghost town at night. It was one reason he'd taken the apartment over one of the new shops. He'd told his folks that he moved off the ranch for the peace and quiet. He didn't want them knowing that his nightmares hadn't stopped. They were getting worse.

A groan from the darkness made him jump. His heart pounded in his throat as he turned to stare into the blackness beyond the edge of the street. The sound definitely hadn't been his imagination. The night was so dark he couldn't see anything after the pavement ended. The sidewalks hadn't been poured yet, some of the streets not yet paved. He heard another sound that appeared to be coming from down the narrow alley between two buildings under construction.

He quickly stepped back to the driver's side of his pickup and grabbed his flashlight. Walking through the glow of his headlights, he headed into the darkness beyond the street. The narrow beam of light skittered to the edge of the pavement and froze on a spot of blood.

Deeper into the dirt alley, the beam came to rest on the woman as she tried to crawl away. She clawed at the ground, clearly exhausted, clearly terrified, before collapsing halfway down the alley.

She wasn't an apparition. And she was alive! He rushed to her. Her forehead was bleeding from a small cut, and her hands and knees were scraped from crawling across the rough pavement and then the dirt to escape. In the flashlight's glow, he saw that her face was bruised from injuries she'd suffered before tonight. From what he could tell, his pickup hadn't hit her.

But there was no doubt that she was terrified. Her eyes widened in horror at the sight of him. A high-pitched keening sound filled the air and she kicked at him and stumbled to her feet. He could see that she was exhausted because she hadn't taken more than few steps when she dropped to her knees and tried to crawl away again.

She was shivering uncontrollably in the tattered sheet wrapped around her. He caught up to her, took off his jacket and put it over her, fearing she was suffering from hypothermia. He could see that her wrists and ankles were chafed where she'd been bound with the duct tape. She was barefoot and naked except for the soiled white sheet she was wrapped in.

"It's all right," he said as he pulled out his cell phone to call for help. "You're all right now. I'm going to get help." She lay breathing hard, collapsed in the dirt. "Can you tell me who did this to you? Miss, can you hear me?" he asked, leaning closer to make sure she was still breathing. Her pale eyes flew open, startling him as much as the high-pitched scream that erupted from her.

As the 911 operator came on the line, he had to yell to be heard over the woman's shrieks. "This is Deputy Marshal Brick Savage," he said as he gave the address, asking for assistance and an ambulance ASAP.

Chapter Two

After very little sleep and an early call from his father the next morning, Brick dressed in his uniform and drove down to the law enforcement building. He was hoping that this would be the day that his father, Marshal Hud Savage, told him he would finally be on active duty. He couldn't wait to get his teeth into something, a real investigation. After finding that woman last night, he wanted more than anything to be the one to get her justice.

"Come in and close the door," his father said before motioning him into a chair across from his desk.

"Is this about the woman I encountered last night?" he asked as he removed his Stetson and dropped into a chair across from him. He'd stayed at the hospital until the doctor had sent him home. When he called this morning, he'd been told that the woman appeared to be in a catatonic state and was unresponsive.

"We have a name on your Jane Doe," his father said now. "Natalie Berkshire."

Brick frowned. The name sounded vaguely familiar. But that wasn't what surprised him. "Already? Her fingerprints?"

Hud nodded and slid a copy of the *Billings Gazette* toward him. He picked it up and saw the headline sprawled across the front page, *Alleged Infant Killer Released for Lack of Evidence*. The newspaper was two weeks old.

Brick felt a jolt rock him back in his chair. "She's *that* woman?" He couldn't help his shock. He thought of the terrified woman who'd crossed in front of his truck last night. Nothing like the woman he remembered seeing on television coming out of the law enforcement building in Billings after being released.

"I don't know what to say." Nor did he know what to think. The woman he'd found had definitely been victimized. He thought he'd saved her. He'd been hell-bent on getting her justice. With his Stetson balanced on his knee, he raked his fingers through his hair.

"I'm trying to make sense of this, as well," his father said. "Since her release, more evidence had come out in former cases. She's now wanted for questioning in more deaths of patients who'd been under her care from not just Montana. Apparently, the moment she was released, she disappeared. Billings PD checked her apartment. It appeared that she'd left in a hurry and hasn't been seen since."

"Until last night when she stumbled in front of my pickup," Brick said. "You think she's been held captive all this time?"

"Looks that way," Hud said. "We found her

older model sedan parked behind the convenience store down on Highway 191. We're assuming she'd stopped for gas. The attendant who was on duty recognized her from a photo. She remembered seeing Natalie at the gas pumps and thinking she looked familiar but couldn't place her at the time. The attendant said a large motor home pulled in and she lost sight of her and didn't see her again."

"When was this?" Brick asked.

"Two weeks ago. Both the back seat and the trunk of her car were full of her belongings."

"So she was running away when she was abducted." Brick couldn't really blame her. "After all the bad publicity, I can see why she couldn't stay in Billings. But taking off like that makes her either look guilty—or scared."

"Or both. This case got a lot of national coverage for months. Unfortunately, her case was tried in the press and she was found guilty. When there wasn't sufficient evidence in the Billings case to prosecute, they had no choice but to let her go. My guess is that someone who didn't like the outcome took the law into his own hands."

Brick nodded. "It would be some coincidence if she was abducted and held by someone who had no idea who she was." He shook his head, remembering the terror he'd seen in her eyes. "What if she's innocent of these crimes?"

"It seems that all of her nursing care positions involved patients with severe health issues," Hud said. "It's no surprise that a lot of the old cases are being reopened now. All of her patients died before she moved on to her next nursing job."

"So foul play was never considered in most of the other deaths?" Brick said. "But it is now even though she was released. No wonder she ran."

His father nodded. "Several of the Billings homicide detectives are on their way. I get the impression they might have discovered more evidence against her. It's possible they plan to arrest her—or at the least, take her into custody for questioning."

Brick rubbed the back of his neck as he tried to imagine the woman he'd found last night as a cold-blooded killer. "And if they don't?"

"Unless one of the other investigations across the country wants her detained, then, when she's well, she'll be released from the hospital and free to go."

"To be on her own knowing there is someone out there who means her harm?" Brick couldn't help being shocked by that. "Someone abducted her, held her captive for apparently weeks and if not tortured her, definitely did a number on her." He couldn't help his warring emotions. The woman might be guilty as sin. Or not. Clearly, she wasn't safe. He'd seen how terrified she'd been last night. *Someone* had found her. He didn't doubt they would again.

"Once the press finds out who the woman is in our hospital, it will be a media circus," his father was saying. "I know you found her, but I'd prefer you stay out of this. However, I'm sure Billings homicide will want to talk to you. This will have to be handled delicately, to say the least."

"You don't think I can do *delicate*?"

The marshal smiled as he leaned back in his chair. "I think you're going to make a damned good deputy marshal, maybe even marshal, in time." In time. Time had suddenly become Brick's enemy. "You've gotten the training," his father continued, "and once you get the last medical release..."

Brick didn't need the reminder of what had happened to him. The fact that he'd almost died wasn't something he'd forgotten. He had the scars to remind him. Those and the nightmares. But he hadn't just been wounded in the mountains of Wyoming and almost died. He'd killed the man who shot him. He wasn't sure which haunted him the most.

He also didn't need another pep talk on being patient until he got a mental health physician to release him for active duty. Until then, he was sentenced to doing menial desk job work.

"I should get going." No matter what his father said, he had to see the woman again. He wasn't scheduled to work until later. He had plenty of time to stop by the hospital before his appointment with the shrink and his desk job shift. But as he started to get to his feet, his father waved him back down.

"Brick, if you're thinking of going by the hospital, you should know that she can't tell you what happened to her or who is responsible. She's in what the doctor called a catatonic or unresponsive state, something often associated with trauma."

"I know, I already called, but I have to see her." He couldn't forget that moment when she'd appeared in front of his headlights. It haunted him—just as the woman did. "I found her. I almost hit her with my pickup. I feel…connected to her."

Brick knew it was a lot more than that. He was going crazy sitting behind a desk, cooling his heels until the shrink said he was ready to get to work. It left him too much time to think.

Not that he would tell his father or the psychiatrist he was required to see later today, but finding that woman last night *had* brought back his ordeal in Wyoming. That was another reason he wanted—needed—to see this through.

MARSHAL HUD SAVAGE leaned forward to study his son. "How are the nightmares?"

Brick shook his head, not meeting his gaze. "No longer a problem."

He watched his son shift on his feet, anxious to get out the door. "Son, you know how happy I was when you wanted the deputy marshal job that was coming open."

"I can do the job, if that's what you're worried about."

"I believe you can, but not yet."

"I'm healed. Doc cleared me weeks ago."

"I'm not talking about your physical injuries. You need clearance from a mental health professional as well, and I heard you missed your last appointment."

Brick swore. "I'm fine. I had a conflict… Besides, is it really necessary after all this time?"

"It is." He was more convinced of that after seeing how personally involved Brick had become with the woman he'd found last night. Although Brick and Angus were identical twins, they were so different it amazed him. Brick had always been the carefree one, hardly ever serious, ready with a joke when he got in trouble. He was also the one who made his mother laugh the most and that meant a lot to Hud.

Dana was delighted to have her son come home six months ago to recuperate. Hud knew she hoped that he'd be staying once he was well. Brick had always taken wrangling jobs with his brother. That was how he'd ended up down in Wyoming. She'd thought maybe she could convince him, like she had Angus, to stay on the ranch and work it with his twin.

So Dana wasn't as pleased that he wanted to follow his father's footsteps into law enforcement. She blamed Hud for making the profession look too glamorous, which had made him laugh. Her dream was that their children would embrace the ranch lifestyle and return to Cardwell Ranch to run it.

But Brick had always stubbornly gone his own way even as a child.

"It wasn't just your body that went through the trauma," Hud said now to his son. "You need to heal. I suspect one of the reasons you're so interested in this case is that finding that woman in the condition she was in brought back what happened to you in Wyoming."

Brick scoffed. "I was *shot*. I wasn't tied up in some basement and abused."

"I don't think you've dealt with how close you

came to dying or the fact that you were forced to take another man's life. It's standard procedure, son. Don't miss today's appointment."

BRICK GLANCED AT the time as he drove to the hospital. There would be hell to pay if he missed his doctor appointment. But he had to at least see the woman again. He felt confused. Not that seeing her lying in the hospital bed would probably help with that confusion.

He still couldn't believe that the woman he'd rescued was the notorious nurse who'd worked as a nanny for a young couple in Billings. The couple's newborn son had multiple life-threatening medical problems. They'd opted to take their son home and be with him for as long as they had.

Natalie Berkshire had sworn that when she came into the nursery she found the baby blue. She'd tried to resuscitate him, screaming for the mother to call 911. But he was gone. An autopsy revealed that the baby had died from lack of oxygen. It wasn't until fibers from the baby's blanket were found in his lungs that Natalie was arrested, and then released when the case against her wasn't strong enough for a conviction.

Now as Brick took the stairs to her floor, he told himself that he was invested in this case whether his father liked it or not. True, he was restless and ached to get back to actively working, but he also wanted to prove to his father that he could do this job.

He knew his dad had had his reservations. All

Brick had known growing up on Cardwell Ranch in the Gallatin Canyon was wrangling horses and cattle. He'd never shown an interest in law enforcement before, so he couldn't blame him for being skeptical at first.

After coming home to recuperate after his ordeal in Wyoming, he'd realized it was time to settle down. When he'd heard about the deputy marshal position coming open, he'd jumped at it. He told himself that he wasn't grabbing up the first thing that came along, as his father feared. Somehow, it felt right.

At least he hoped so as he came out of the stairwell on Natalie Berkshire's floor. He was only a little winded by the hike up the stairs, but he was getting stronger every day. Physically, he was recovering nicely, his doctor had said. If it wasn't for the nightmares…

Walking down the hall, he was glad to see the deputy stationed outside her door. He'd been relieved last night when his father had assigned a deputy to guard her after the lab techs had taken what evidence they could gather—including her fingerprints, which ID'd her.

Brick had feared she was still in danger from whoever had held her captive. At the time, he hadn't known just how much danger this woman was in—or what she was running from.

After being raised in a house with his marshal father, he believed in innocence until proven guilty. If this woman was guilty, she deserved a trial. But even as Brick thought it, he wondered if she could get one anywhere in this country after all the publicity.

As he approached her room, he hoped his father hadn't told the guard not to let him in.

"Hey, Jason," Brick said as he approached the deputy sitting outside her door. The marshal department in Big Sky was small, so he knew most everyone by name even though he was new. And everyone knew him. Being the marshal's son was good and bad. He wouldn't get any special treatment—not from his father. If anything, Hud Savage would be tougher on him. But he couldn't have anyone thinking he was special because of his last name.

"That must have been something, finding her like you did," Jason said.

Brick nodded as he looked toward her closed door. "Any trouble?"

"Not a peep out of her."

"No one's come by looking for her?" Brick knew how news traveled in this small canyon town. He feared that whoever had held the woman captive would hear that she'd been taken to the hospital. The hospital was small and busy during the summer season. If someone were determined to get in, they would find a way.

"Nope."

Brick heard a sound inside the room and looked quizzically to the guard.

"Nurse." The deputy grinned. "Good-looking one too. I'd let her take my vitals."

Brick smiled, shaking his head at the man, and

pushed open the door. As he did, the nurse beside the bed who'd been leaning over the patient now looked up in alarm.

He took in the scene in that split second as the door closed behind him. The guard was right. The nurse was a stunner, blonde with big blue eyes.

"I didn't mean to startle you," he said as he stepped deeper into the room, sensing that something was wrong.

"You didn't." The nurse began to nervously straighten the patient's sheet before she turned toward him to leave. He realized with a start that the patient had been saying something as he walked in. He'd seen Natalie's lips moving. Her eyes had been open, but were now closed. Had he only imagined that she'd spoken? How was that possible if the woman was catatonic and nonresponsive?

Also, when he'd come in and the nurse had been leaning over the patient, she'd clearly been intent on what Natalie was saying. She'd straightened so quickly as he'd come in. But before that, he'd seen something in the nurse's face…

The hair rose on the back of his neck.

"I heard the patient was catatonic. Any change?" he asked.

"No, I'm afraid not," the nurse said and started toward him on her way out of the room.

"Please don't let me stop you from what you were doing."

"I'm finished." She had to walk right past him to get out the door. As she approached, he looked at her more closely. If he was right and had heard Natalie speak, then the nurse had lied about there being no change. But why would she lie?

Looking past her, he noticed a pillow on the floor where she'd been standing. It had apparently fallen off the bed. It seemed strange that she hadn't taken the time to pick it up and put it back on the patient's bed. But that wasn't half as odd as her apparent need to get out of this room as quickly as possible.

His gaze shot to her uniform. No name tag.

Even as he raised his arm to stop her, he still couldn't be sure of what he'd thought he'd seen—and heard. But he couldn't shake the feeling that something was very wrong here. That he'd walked into something… "Hold up just a minute."

The moment he reached for the woman, she jerked back her arm and spun to face him. Before he could react, she jammed her forearm into his throat. As he gasped for air, she kicked him in the groin.

Even as the pain doubled him over, he grabbed for her, but she slipped through his fingers. He tried to call to the deputy stationed outside the door, but he had no breath, no air, no voice. All he could do for a few moments was watch her push out of the hospital room door.

Limping to the door after her, he found the deputy out in the hall talking to the doctor. The hallway was empty. He tried to speak but nothing came out as he bent over, hands on his knees, and sucked in painful breaths.

The woman in the nurse's uniform was long gone.

Chapter Three

The marshal sat back in his chair and listened as his son told him again what had happened at the hospital. Brick had called it in on his way to his psychiatrist's office. Hud had been glad to see that his son hadn't used what happened to him at the hospital as an excuse to get out of his doctor's appointment.

Hud had been having trouble believing this story. The doctor had insisted that Natalie Berkshire was still catatonic and questioned if the deputy had actually heard her speak. But the description of the nurse Brick had seen didn't match that of any woman who worked at the hospital. Five-foot-five, blonde, big blue eyes, a knockout.

"So you didn't actually witness her doing anything to the patient," Hud said now. He could see how upset his son was. Finding the woman last night had clearly shaken him and now this. As Brick had said, he felt responsible for her, something he admired in his son. But Brick couldn't take on this kind of responsibility every time he helped someone as a deputy marshal. He wondered again if this job was right for him. Or if his son was ready for any of this after what had happened to him.

"No, I didn't actually see her threaten the patient, but there was a pillow on the floor and she was acting...suspicious. Also, I swear, I heard the patient say something to her. If you'd seen the nurse's reaction to whatever Natalie was saying..."

"But you didn't hear the actual words?" Hud asked.

Brick shook his head. "She was whispering and the nurse was leaning over her. My attention was on the nurse and her expression. I'm telling you, the nurse was looking down at the patient as if she wanted to kill her. But whatever Natalie was saying appeared to have...shocked her."

"You got all of this in an instant when you walked into the room?"

His son shrugged. "It was just a feeling I got when I walked in that something was wrong. So maybe I was paying more attention. I know what I saw *and* what I heard. If I hadn't gone in when I did, who knows what the woman would have done."

Hud groaned inwardly. If they arrested every person who acted suspicious there would be no room in the jails for the true criminals. He said as much to his son.

"She was pretending to be a nurse. Not to mention the fact that she attacked me, an officer of the law. Isn't that enough?"

"You said you grabbed her arm as she was starting to leave. Did you announce yourself as a deputy marshal?"

Brick sighed. "No, but I was wearing my uniform, and if you'd seen the way she was looking down at the patient..."

Hud admitted it sounded more than a little suspicious. "Okay, the hospital staff will be watching for her should she try to get into the woman's hospital room again. She could just be a reporter looking for a story. Brick?" He could see how rattled his son was. All the talk in the marshal's department would be about this case. "I want you to take the rest of the week off. I'll talk to your doctor at the beginning of next week. If he gives the all clear..."

His son chuckled and shook his head. "By then, Natalie Berkshire will either be arrested and hauled off for questioning, or gone."

"It's for the best."

BRICK SWORE UNDER his breath. "I know what I saw and what I heard. That woman posing as a nurse was in that room to kill Natalie. But whatever Natalie said to her made her hesitate. Then I walked in... What if this nurse is the one who's been holding Natalie captive?"

"I'll find out the truth," his father said. "I wasn't just suggesting that you take the rest of the week off. It's an order. Go camping. You're too involved in this case. Take advantage of this time off. Hike up into the mountains to a nice lake and camp for a few days. I brought you on too soon and I'm sorry about that."

He was about to argue when his father's phone rang. He wasn't leaving. Not until he convinced the marshal that he couldn't get rid of him that easily.

Then he saw his father's expression as he finished his phone conversation and hung up. What had happened? *Something.* "I'm meeting with a psychiatrist. I'm doing everything you asked. So stop trying to get rid of me. Tell me what's happened. You know I'll find out one way or another anyway. And if you don't want me trying to find out on my own—"

With a sigh, Hud said, "From your description and surveillance cameras at the hospital, they've been able to make a possible ID of the woman pretending to be a nurse. Her name is Maureen 'Mo' Mortensen."

"She must have some connection to the case," Brick said.

His father nodded. "The baby in Natalie Berkshire's care when he was allegedly murdered was her sister's."

Brick swore. "That would explain why she was standing over Natalie staring down at her as if she wanted to kill her."

"What makes this case more tragic is that Maureen Mortensen's sister committed suicide just days after Natalie was released."

"Tricia Colton," he said. "I remember seeing the husband on the news. He blamed Natalie for destroying his family. His wife had hung herself in the family garage. So Maureen Mortensen is her sister? Is she in the military or something? She attacked me as if she was trained in combat."

"She was a homicide detective in Billings."

"Was?"

"She's been temporarily suspended."

"Why?" Brick asked.

"I suspect it has something to do with her conflict of interest in the case. Apparently, she had been doing some investigating on her own before Natalie was released. She was ordered off the case, but refused to listen." He gave Brick a meaningful look.

Brick ignored it as he thought of what he'd seen at the hospital. "She wasn't the one who abducted and held Natalie Berkshire captive."

"What makes you say that?"

"Just a feeling I got that she hadn't seen Natalie for a while." He felt his father's gaze on him. "What?"

"Always trust your instincts."

He smiled. It was the most affirmation his father had given him since he'd signed on as a new deputy. "Thanks."

"But that doesn't mean that you aren't wrong."

He thought about it for a moment. "This woman, Mo, wants her dead—not tied up and tortured."

"You have no evidence that Mortensen was trying to kill the woman," his father pointed out. "Also, the doctor said that Natalie Berkshire couldn't have spoken to the woman. She's still nonresponsive."

Brick shook his head. "I swear I heard her. What's more, the fake nurse-slash-cop heard her."

"I've put a BOLO out on Mortensen to have her picked up for questioning."

"How about for assaulting a lawman?"

"It's enough to at least hold her for a while. I'm sure Billings PD will want to talk to her once they get here. But I do wonder how it was that she found out Natalie Berkshire was in the Big Sky hospital," his father said. "Unless she's been looking for her since her suspension—and Natalie's disappearance."

"Well, now she's found her," Brick said. "I wouldn't be surprised if she tries to get to her again."

Brick was still trying to process everything his father had told him. He'd been so sure that Natalie Berkshire had been the victim and that Maureen Mortensen was the criminal. Even if his father picked up the blonde cop, his instincts told him that she wouldn't be behind bars long. When she got out, he put his money on her going after Natalie Berkshire.

Maybe his father was right, and Maureen "Mo" Mortensen wouldn't have killed the woman lying in the hospital bed if he hadn't walked in. But from her expression, she'd darn sure wanted to.

"I bet the cop hasn't gone far," he said, wondering where she'd been staying. Probably at one of the local motels. He said as much to his father.

"I know she hurt your ego and you might want to go after her yourself because of it, but you're staying out of this. I shouldn't have put you on the schedule until we had the release from the mental health doctor. Don't argue with me about this. And come to dinner tonight. Your mother would love to see you."

Brick rose and started for the door.

"One more thing," his father said behind him. "I'm going to need your badge, star and weapon."

Brick turned to look at him as he slowly took off his star, pulled his badge and unsnapped his holster and laid all three on his father's desk.

"You can order me to take a few days off, but you can't make me go camping. Just as you can't order me to come to dinner." He turned and walked out, telling himself that becoming a deputy and working under his father was a huge mistake.

MAUREEN "MO" MORTENSEN wiped the steam off the cracked mirror and locked eyes with the woman in the glass, but only for an instant. She didn't like what she saw in her blue eyes. It scared her. Sometimes she didn't recognize herself and the woman she'd become.

Splashing cold water on her face, she thought of what had happened at the hospital. She'd come close to getting caught. But that wasn't all she'd come close to. If that deputy marshal hadn't walked in when he had…

She was still shaken, not just by Natalie's condition. She felt sick to her stomach at the memory. She'd looked down at the woman's bruised face. It had been true, what she'd heard. Natalie had been abducted and held prisoner. She'd thought she couldn't feel sympathy for what the woman must have gone through, but she'd been wrong. She didn't wish that sort of treatment on anyone, even a murderer.

For a long moment, she'd stood next to Natalie's bed, staring down at her. Had she been trying to see the monster behind the skin and bone? When the woman had opened her eyes, it had startled her. She'd read on her chart that she was catatonic. But looking into the Natalie's eyes, she'd seen fear, surprise and then something even more shocking—resignation.

Natalie had known why Mo had sneaked into the hospital dressed as a nurse. Would Mo have gone through with it? She might never know because the woman's words had stopped her cold.

Mo still felt stunned. By the time the words had registered, the deputy had come into the hospital room. She'd wanted to scream because she'd known that her chance to question Natalie had passed. All she could do was clear out of there with the hope that she could get another chance to question Natalie alone.

It surprised her that now she wanted the truth more than she wanted vengeance.

Unfortunately, she also now had the law looking for her. Getting free of the deputy had been instinctive. How could she reach Natalie again, though, with even more people looking for her? That cocky deputy marshal would be after her.

She pushed the thought away. She had more problems than some deputy marshal. Her body ached. Even when she could find the haven of sleep, she often woke bone-weary, more tired than she'd ever been. In her dreams, she'd been chasing Natalie Berkshire for months. In real life, it had only been since the woman had been released from custody—two weeks ago.

Today was the closest she'd come to finishing this. That moment of hesitation had cost her. She remembered looking into those pale hazel eyes. Natalie had known exactly who she was. The words she'd spoken weren't those of a mad woman. Nor of a liar. That was what had made them so shocking.

Natalie had known why Mo was there. She'd been ready to die. Because she knew she deserved it? Or because she knew she couldn't keep running?

In all the time she'd been a cop, Mo had never hesitated when everything was on the line, and yet earlier… If Natalie really had been catatonic… If she hadn't opened her eyes. If she hadn't spoken… The thought chilled her. Would she have gone through with what she'd planned?

Shaking her head at her disappointment in not being able to question Natalie after the woman had dropped that bombshell, she threw what little she'd brought into her suitcase. She didn't have time for introspection or recriminations. Or to try to analyze what the woman said or what it could mean.

She would get another chance to talk to Natalie—hopefully alone. She had to. Natalie had evaded almost everyone—except whoever had abducted her. Mo thought about the woman's bruises. Whoever had found her didn't want her dead. They wanted to punish her and had.

The thought pained her. It wasn't as if the woman was a stranger. She'd known Natalie. Or at least she thought she'd known her. Mo had spent time at that house with her sister and brother-in-law and their live-in nanny. She'd watched the woman not just with little Joey, but with her sister. Tricia had bonded with Natalie. The three women had become friends. Mo had liked the quiet, pleasant Natalie Berkshire. What's more, she'd seen that her sister had liked the woman as well and vice versa. Natalie, during those months, had become part of the family.

That thought hurt more than she wanted to admit. They'd all trusted the woman—even Mo. She *had* to talk to Natalie again. If there was even a chance that what she'd said might be true…

It surprised her how just a few words from the woman could change everything. When a friend at the police department had called her to say that something had come up on the scanner, she'd driven to Big Sky as fast as she could. The marshal in Big Sky said he'd called Billings PD to let them know that he had Natalie Berkshire after she'd apparently escaped after being abducted. Mo had arrived late last night. When she'd stopped on the edge of Big Sky to get something to eat at an all-night convenience store and deli, she'd overheard a table of nurses talking. One night shift nurse had described the woman who'd been brought in.

Mo had felt a chill ripple through her. From the description, she'd known it was true. The patient was Natalie, no matter how bizarre the circumstances that had landed her in the Big Sky hospital.

She'd listened to the night nurse talking in a low,

confidential tone and caught enough to know that the woman brought in had been held captive for an unknown amount of time. She heard the words *duct tape, bruises, a torn and filthy sheet.*

She'd also heard that a deputy marshal by the name of Brick Savage had found her and gotten her to the hospital—the closest hospital in the area—where she had originally been listed as a Jane Doe. Until her prints had come back.

This morning, Mo had picked up scubs and Crocs at the discount store. She'd walked into the hospital as if she knew what she was doing. The older woman at the information desk only smiled as she went by.

Upstairs, she'd found Natalie's room by looking for the deputy she'd heard had been parked outside it. All she'd had to do was give him a smile and walk right into the room.

One glance toward the bed and she'd known she was about to get her chance for justice. It was Natalie, and given the shape she was in, Mo knew that someone else had caught up to her first. She'd suspected for some time that she wasn't the only one looking for the woman.

She'd thought she'd known exactly what she would do when she found her. She owed it to her sister and to Thomas, her sister's still grieving husband, and to little Joey, their infant son. She'd kept what she was doing from Thomas. He'd been so devastated by the loss of his son and wife that he'd begged Mo to let it go.

"I can't take anymore," he'd cried when she'd argued that she had to find evidence to stop Natalie.

"But she'll kill again," she'd argued.

"For the love of God, Mo. I never want to hear that woman's name again. For months Tricia and I thought we'd get justice. When Natalie was released..." Tricia had killed herself. "I need to make peace with this. I hope you can, too."

She had known that she wouldn't find peace until Natalie was either dead or behind bars. She had been determined that Natalie would not destroy another family.

But then Natalie had opened her eyes and said the only words that could have changed her mind—even temporarily.

Mo moved to the motel room door, suitcase in hand. She looked back to make sure she hadn't left anything behind. She figured that it wouldn't take long, between the deputy who'd gotten a good look at her and the surveillance cameras, before they knew her name. That would definitely make finding her easier since she'd used her real name when she'd checked into the motel.

She wouldn't make that mistake again, she thought. Nor would it be a good idea to stay in any one place too long. Not that she was planning on this taking any longer than necessary. She would get back into the hospital. Security would be tighter. They would be watching for her.

Mo knew that the best thing she could do was wait until Natalie was released, but she had no idea when that would be. Also, she knew that Billings homicide were on their way—because some old cases were now being reopened and other departments were anxious to talk to Natalie. If they didn't arrest her and Natalie was released from the hospital, she would run like a scared rabbit and be all that much harder to catch.

She picked up her purse on the table by the door, swung the strap over her shoulder and, shifting the suitcase in her hand, reached with the other one to open the door. She already had a plan simmering at the back of her mind, a way to get into the hospital again.

She'd go to the store, get some supplies to change her appearance. This time she'd go in not as a nurse, but as a male workman instead. She would bluff her way in and no matter what she had to do, she'd get into Natalie's room. She would get the truth out of the woman and then…

Mo refused to think beyond that point. What she had in mind had never sat easy with her. But she felt she had no choice. She was convinced of what would happen if Natalie was as guilty as she believed and she didn't stop her.

With purse and suitcase in hand, she opened the door and stepped out of the motel room—right into a pair of deputies…and handcuffs.

Chapter Four

Angry and frustrated, Brick was even more determined to find out the truth about Natalie Berkshire. He knew he was taking one hell of a chance, but he drove through town to Highway 191 to the convenience store where Natalie Berkshire had allegedly been abducted. Inside, he bought an ice cream cone and asked the clerk if she'd been on duty that day when the woman had been abducted. She hadn't, but she told him everything the other clerk had told her.

Behind the wheel of his pickup again, he sat and ate his ice cream cone. The appointment with the psychiatrist had gone better than he'd hoped. He liked the man and thought his father was right. Talking about what had happened up on the mountain might get rid of the nightmares. He would gladly see the last of them. They were too vivid and bizarre, a jumble of confusing, frightening images that finally woke him in a cold sweat.

He knew he shouldn't have been surprised, but after talking about it and everything else that had happened in the past twenty-four hours, he felt drained. He had gotten hardly any sleep last night after Natalie Berkshire stumbled into his headlights. He'd been coming from the late shift. Finding her had added even more dark images to his sleep.

Now he couldn't help thinking about her or the blonde cop, Mo. Was Natalie a killer? Or was she innocent? Was Mo a vigilante cop with a need for vengeance? Or was she like a lot of people who feared Natalie had gotten away with murder and would kill again if not stopped?

Two women. One set on escape. The other on closure. But someone else, who was set on dispensing his own brand of justice, had already abducted Natalie Berkshire. Would they have eventually killed her if she hadn't escaped?

And what would the rogue cop do now if she wasn't found and stopped?

Brick knew the answers were out there and he desperately wanted to find them. He still swore that Natalie had spoken to the cop. Said something that had stopped her. Something in addition to continuing to swear she was innocent. The more he thought about it, he realized that the two had known each other before the murder. Natalie had been her sister's nanny. Who knows how close they might have been.

What a complicated, intriguing case. It did make him wonder who was innocent. It also made him want to help solve it more than he'd ever wanted anything.

He sat in his truck for a few minutes after eating his ice cream, trying to decide what to do—if anything. He was exhausted from everything that had happened, not just in the past twenty-four hours. As he shifted in the seat, he felt his harmonica in his pocket and pulled it out. He'd carried the musical instrument from the day his grandfather Angus had given it to him. It had taken him a lot longer than he'd hoped to learn how to play it. But he'd stayed with it until he'd finally mastered a few of his favorite tunes. As was his character, he wasn't one to give up.

That was why it hurt so much to realize that he hadn't played the harmonica since the events up on the mountain in Wyoming. Nor did he want to. He put it back in his pocket and had to swallow the lump in his throat. Maybe he wasn't as well as he thought he was. Not yet. But he would be.

He needed to solve this puzzle for his own sake. It seemed to him that at least two people were after Natalie Berkshire. One was a suspended cop. The other was the person who'd caught up to her, abducted her and abused her. The clerk at the convenience store had said that all the other clerk had seen was a large motor home driven by an elderly man.

Starting his pickup's engine, he realized a place to begin would be finding where Natalie had been held. He'd discovered her on his street, but he knew she could have come from anywhere. All he knew for certain was the first spot she'd appeared.

He drove to his neighborhood. The businesses were all open now, the streets busy since it was June in Montana and the beginning of tourist season. He circled the block, extending his circles further out with each lap.

If he were going to abduct someone he would need a safe place to keep the person. Somewhere away from other people. In a way this could be the perfect neighborhood—at least at night. But during the day, there were too many construction workers around as well as tourists and shop owners and workers. Also, most of the new structures didn't have basements, so where had Natalie been held?

Brick had just turned down another street when he saw that he was running out of town. The landscape around Big Sky was sagebrush before the terrain went up into towering pine-covered mountains. The Gallatin River cut through it, forming the deep, often dark canyon. A sign caught his eye. Campground.

He felt as if he'd been touched with a cattle prod. The clerk at the convenience store had seen a motor home pull in when she'd lost sight of Natalie. He'd at first assumed that the motor home had blocked her view of whoever had taken the woman. But what if whoever had taken the woman had been driving the motor home?

He pointed his truck down the road to the south, but he hadn't gone far when he heard the bleep of a siren. Glancing in his rearview mirror, he saw the quick flash of the light bar on the patrol SUV that was now behind him.

With a curse, he pulled over and got out to walk back to talk to his father.

"I know what you're doing," Hud said with a sigh.

Brick wasn't going to deny it. "I think I know where she was held. That motor home that pulled in. I think she was being held at the campground up the road."

His father shook his head in exasperation before saying, "Get in. I was just headed there. How did I know you'd be going my way?"

Brick grinned at him as he slid in. "You're psychic. I remember when Angus and I were boys. You were always one step ahead of us."

"And you were always the ringleader and the one that never did what you were told, let alone listened to any advice I gave you."

"Her feet were covered in dirt from walking through soil before she reached my neighborhood."

His father didn't respond, but he saw a small smile curve the man's lips as he drove and Brick buckled up. The campground was just off Highway 191 in stands of pines that offered privacy for campers. It also allowed self-contained rigs to stay for several weeks for free because there were no outhouses or water. Just as there was no campground host. The isolated campsites were large enough to accommodate a motor home.

Even this time of day with the sun high in the sky, the canyon was cold and dark. Brick had been away from home for so long he'd forgotten just how tight the Gallatin Canyon was in places. Highway 191 was a narrow strip of pavement hemmed in on one side by the river and mountain cliffs on the other. It was often filled with deep shadows and stayed cool even in the summer because of a lack of sunshine. During the last widening of the highway, small pullouts had been added for slower vehicles to pull over to let others pass when there was room.

June weather was often unpredictable. It wasn't uncommon for it to snow and end up closing some roads. That was why July and August were the big travel months in this part of Montana. Because of that, the campground would have been relatively empty the past few weeks.

Only two rigs were still parked among the trees. One was a pickup and camper. The other an SUV pulling a small travel trailer.

The marshal pulled in, turned off the engine and said, "Stay here and try to remember that you're just along for the ride."

Brick watched his father unsnap the weapon on his hip as he climbed out and walked toward to the small trailer. If Marshal Hud Savage was anything, he was cautious, and with reason. They had no idea who had taken Natalie Berkshire prisoner or how many people might be in on it.

Over the patrol SUV radio came a call. Brick picked it up. "Deputy Brick Savage."

The dispatcher said, "Just wanted to let the marshal know that a couple of deputies just brought in Maureen Mortensen."

They'd found the blonde cop already? "I'll let him know." As he got off the radio, he saw his father standing at the trailer door. Sometimes he forgot how large a man Hud Savage was. He had always been broad-shouldered and strong as an ox. Even at almost retirement age, he was still a big man, still impressive in not just his size. He'd always been good at what he did as well, Brick thought with a flood of emotion. He wanted so badly to follow in this man's footsteps, but worried he could never fill his boots.

He watched as a rather rotund man answered the marshal's knock.

Popping open his door so he could hear, Brick listened to his father questioning the man before moving on to the next rig.

Brick couldn't hear as well this time, but he saw the man who answered the marshal's knock point to a space at the back of the campground. His father nodded, then headed in that direction.

Brick got out of the patrol SUV and followed him into a stand of dense pines. If the motor home had been parked here, it wouldn't have been visible from the highway. Nor was it near any other campsite. Even if Natalie had screamed bloody murder, she might not have been heard. But he doubted that whomever had taken her had allowed her to scream at all.

He stopped short when he saw what his father was doing—snapping photographs with his phone of the tire tracks left in the soft earth. This was where the motor home had been. But had Natalie been inside it?

"A call just came in on the radio," he told the marshal. "A couple of deputies picked up Maureen Mortensen." He wasn't sure what response he was expecting, but his father only nodded.

Without a word, they walked back to the patrol SUV and climbed inside before his father said, "You need to learn how to take orders." Hud started the engine. "You always were the stubborn one."

Brick chuckled at that. "Just like my father and grandfather, I'm told."

"Well, at least your namesake grandfather." Brick had heard stories about his grandfather Brick Savage, the former marshal. If half of the stories were true, then his father and the former marshal had butted heads regularly.

"Any update on Natalie?" he asked him now.

"Still catatonic." His father sighed, picked up his radio and called in a description of the motor home that the man in the camper had given him. It sounded like one of those rental motor homes. Older driver. Only description was elderly and gray.

If Natalie had been held in the motor home, the driver could be miles from here by now—or parked at the hospital. His father obviously thought the same thing as he asked that a deputy watch for a motor home at the hospital parking lot and ordered that another deputy go to work calling motor home rentals in the area.

They drove in silence back to where Brick had left his pickup. As he started to climb out, his father said, "Deputy, you want this job? Take a week. I don't want to see you again unless it's at your mother's dining room table. And stay clear of Billings PD's case. Got that?"

"Got it."

As he closed the door, Brick heard a call come in over the radio that all law enforcement available were needed for a three-vehicle pileup in the canyon twenty miles south of Big Sky. His father sped off, leaving him standing next to his pickup.

Brick knew he should go camping. Go back into the mountains and not come out until his next doctor's appointment. But as he watched his father's patrol SUV disappear over the rise, he realized this was his chance to go to the hospital and see Natalie. Maybe she was catatonic. Maybe she wasn't. He knew that he'd heard her say something. There was only one way to prove it.

His father was closing in on the theory that she was abducted by a person driving a motor home. It wouldn't be long before the marshal made an arrest. Meanwhile, the Billings homicide detectives should be arriving at any time—if they hadn't already been to the hospital.

And down at the jail there was a blonde cop with a nasty kick locked up behind bars. He wondered what she'd have to say for herself. His groin still hurt, not to mention his bruised ego. He realized that there was nothing he would enjoy more than seeing her behind bars.

Chapter Five

Mo couldn't believe her luck. She'd been arrested on a charge she could wiggle out of the moment she went before a judge, and these backwoods lawmen had to know that. But how long would that take?

She could feel the clock ticking. Once Natalie was released from the hospital, she would be gone again, only this time, she wouldn't make the same mistakes. She could disappear down a rat hole and might not surface for months, even years. By then she would have had numerous jobs. Which meant numerous victims. Mo couldn't let that happen any more than she could let Natalie get away without having the chance to talk to her one more time.

As it stood now, there was no proof that she'd been at the hospital with any felonious intentions. All they had her on was pretending to be a nurse. Given her connection to Natalie Berkshire, the law could try to make something out of that. But ultimately, they wouldn't be able to hold her on any of it—except for her attack on the deputy marshal, Brick Savage—

the man who'd found Natalie after her escape from whoever had abducted her.

Mo paced in her cell. She kept thinking about standing over the woman's bed, hearing the hoarse whisper, feeling the woman's words hit her like a hollow-point slug to her chest. She'd had her right where she wanted her. The truth had been within her reach.

Natalie would run the moment she was released from the hospital. But what was she running from? The law? Her own guilt? Fear? Or this thing she'd kept secret?

At the sound of the door into the cell area opening, she turned to see Deputy Marshal Brick Savage come in and head toward her. She groaned inwardly. Of course he would come to gloat.

When he stopped at her cell door, she warned herself to be cool even as she wanted to wipe that grin off his face. He was enjoying how the tables had turned a little too much. Earlier, she'd felt guilty for attacking him. Right now, not so much.

"Enjoying your stay here?" he asked, shoving back his Stetson to expose a pair of very blue eyes fringed in dark lashes.

"Not really." He was more handsome than she'd taken the time to notice at the hospital. Handsome, well-built and physically fit. And he was clearly looking for a fight. She could tell she'd banged up his ego more than his body.

"You go by Mo?" he asked.

She waited, fairly sure she already knew what

had brought him here. She just wondered how long it would take him to get to the point.

Fortunately, it wasn't long. "Look, I know you were planning to kill her earlier in the hospital—just as I know she told you something," he said.

She wanted to say, "Prove it!" but thought better of it. Antagonizing a deputy, let alone the son of the marshal, was probably not in her best interests—even out here in the sticks. Maybe especially out here in the sticks.

"I'm sorry if there was a misunderstanding at the hospital," she said with cavity-inducing sweetness.

He laughed, a beguiling sound. "Oh, I understood you just fine. I saw the way you were looking at Natalie Berkshire. Like you wanted to kill her."

"Fortunately, that's not against the law."

"Attacking an officer of the law is."

She tried not to smile. "I didn't realize you were a lawman."

"The uniform probably threw you," he said sarcastically.

She shrugged. "I thought you were a lecherous security guard."

His blue eyes narrowed, but he smiled.

"You did grab me, and you didn't announce who you were. It was a innocent mistake."

"I doubt there is anything innocent about you," he said.

Mo chuckled at that, thinking how true that was. She was no longer the naive woman who'd believed in the law. That had changed everything about her.

She was more daring in every aspect, she realized, as if she had nothing left to lose. In the past, she would have been more careful around a deputy who had her locked up behind bars. Heck, she would have been maybe even a little tongue-tied around a cowboy as handsome as this one. But right now she didn't feel shy or cowed in the least.

She met his Montana-sky-blue gaze, so much deeper and darker than her own. "You're new at this, aren't you? Green as springtime in the Rockies."

His brows furrowed. "Seasoned or not, I'm still a deputy—"

"On medical leave. I also heard that you're the one who found her last night," Mo said. She didn't want to argue semantics. She didn't have time for it.

He eyed her sharply. "Sorry it wasn't you who found her?"

She was, but she wasn't about to admit it to him. "You haven't asked if I was the one who abducted her."

"I don't believe you are. Not your style."

Mo raised a brow and couldn't help but chuckle. "You think you know my style after one…confrontation? I must have made quite an impact on you."

To her surprise, he chuckled, as well. "You could say that. It's why I was anxious to see you—behind bars."

She liked that he could joke. She also liked that he was smart. He'd spotted her quickly for the fraud she was at the hospital. Too quickly. She was curious, though, why he was really here. Just to taunt her? Or did he want something, as she suspected? It was clear that he thought he knew her. That was almost laughable. He had no idea.

"What did she say to you?" he asked.

She felt his gaze on her, a welding torch of heat and intensity.

"She said something to you," he continued. "I heard her."

"I'm not sure what you thought you heard, but the patient, I'm told, is in a catatonic state, unable to speak." She was still dealing with Natalie's words. They'd been private, disarming, horrifying if true. She wasn't about to share them with anyone, especially this half deputy.

"What she said got one hell of a reaction from you," he said as if he hadn't heard her denial. "It stopped you from killing her."

She said nothing, surprised to be hearing the truth in his words. She had gone to the hospital to get an answer to one question and then, well, then, she planned to make sure Natalie never destroyed another family again.

"Sorry, but I don't believe you," the deputy said. "You were leaning over her. I saw her lips moving. I heard her whispering something to you. I want to know why her words made you change your mind."

She started to argue that he had no idea what was in her mind—and even if he did, he couldn't prove it, but he cut her off.

"You want out of this cell? Tell me the truth."

"The truth?" she mocked. "The truth is that Natalie Berkshire is guilty as sin."

"You can prove that?"

"It will get proved, but unfortunately, not before someone else dies because our judicial system takes so long."

"I'm still waiting to hear what she said to you," he said, cocking his head to study her with those intense blue eyes of his.

Mo pulled her gaze away first. She didn't want to tell this cocky cowboy deputy anything. She'd overheard the nurses talking about him last night at the deli. The cowboy had reputation with the women and yet women still seemed to be attracted to him, knowing that he might break their hearts. Good thing he wasn't her type.

"I'm guessing that what Natalie said had something to do with your sister." When she said nothing, he added, "Tricia, isn't that right?"

Her pulse pounded in her ears. Had he heard Natalie say Tricia's name? She groaned inwardly. Natalie Berkshire wasn't just a killer. She was a psychopath who manipulated people. Look how she'd deceived Tricia and her husband, Thomas, and especially Mo herself. Wasn't that the part that kept her up at night?

Trust didn't come easy for her and yet Natalie had gained her trust, and in a very short time. Natalie had walked into their family and become a part of it. Mo had felt as if she'd always known the woman—that was how comfortable she'd been in her presence. Mo didn't make friends easily, but she did make them for life.

When she'd first heard that homicide was being called in, that little Joey was believed to have been smothered, that Natalie was their number one suspect, she hadn't believed it. She'd seen Natalie with Joey. Seen how careful she was with him since his health was so precarious.

But there had been only one other person in that house that afternoon and it was Tricia. According to her sister, she'd been upstairs asleep and had only come down when she'd heard Natalie screaming. It was no wonder the woman had been arrested. Who else could have killed Joey?

That was why Mo had come here to end this nightmare. For weeks she'd rationalized what she had planned, no matter how crazy it seemed most days. Now, she looked the deputy in the eye and told the truth based on what she knew at this moment. "She'll kill again. Unless she's stopped."

"You just know that, right?" he asked, his gaze intent on her. "You have no idea if that is true or not or even if she is the killer." She didn't bother to answer. "Okay, let's say you're right. How exactly do you plan to stop her?"

"That is the question, isn't it?"

"It seems pretty simple. You're no longer a cop—"

"I'm only suspended," she said in her defense, but wondered how long before they found out what she was up to and fired her.

"My point is," he continued, "you have no authority to take her in, and I understand there are no charges pending against her at this point—only suspicions. So why do this? As a homicide detective you know what will happen if you kill her in cold blood."

"You and I wouldn't have been having this discussion only a few months ago. Since then, things have gotten…complicated."

"You're a vigilante cop upset with the system. Doesn't seem all that complicated. Why take it on yourself? I understand that since Natalie was released, other law enforcement departments are reviewing deaths where the woman might have been involved. If she's guilty, it will be just a matter of time before she's under arrest again and a jury will decide," he said.

Mo let out a snort. "What you say may be true, but there isn't time to prove you wrong." She flipped her hair back and met his gaze, narrowing those tropical-sea-blue eyes on him. "When Natalie gets out of that hospital she'll run. She'll be looking for her next job. Her next victim. Someone has to stop her."

"If she's guilty." He was studying her. She felt the burn of his gaze on her skin. "Admit it. You're having your doubts, especially after what she said to you. I saw your reaction. Tell me and I'll get out of here."

She snorted at that. "You're wrong. Nothing Natalie could ever say would convince me that she isn't a killer. So I guess you and I have nothing more to say to each other." She turned her back on the cowboy deputy.

"You change your mind, you let me know."

Brick studied the woman a few moments longer. She had her slim back to him now, her head held high, radiating self-confidence and righteousness. He remembered what the deputy outside Natalie's hospital room door had said about the blonde. At the hospital, he hadn't had the time to get a really good look at her. She was definitely attractive from her thick blond hair that fell over one sea-blue eye before dropping in an asymmetrical cut to her shoulders to her slim, clearly physically fit body. He hadn't known what to expect on actually meeting her, but it was clear to him that she was sharp. She didn't come across as some crackpot on a mission.

Yet while her original intention seemed perfectly clear to him, something had changed when Natalie Berkshire had spoken to her. That intrigued him. Mo hadn't made any bones about her belief that Natalie was guilty. What could the nanny have said to her that would keep her from doing something that she said she was still committed to finishing?

He thought of the pillow on the floor, convinced that his walking into the room wasn't what had stopped her. But he also couldn't imagine what Natalie could have said.

He'd seen the conviction still in Mo's eyes. She wouldn't stop until she found the woman and ended this—one way or another. And like Natalie, soon this woman, too, would be free to do just that.

And that was what had him worried as he left and drove toward the hospital. Mo Mortensen's certainty that Natalie would kill again had him rattled. He was even more anxious to see Natalie Berkshire after talking to the cop. He needed to decide for himself if she was a monster or a victim.

Also, he wanted know exactly what Natalie had said to her, because he no longer believed the woman was catatonic. He could even understand why she was faking it. She was running scared. It was why she'd bailed out of Billings—only to get caught by someone he suspected had been seeking his own kind of justice. Natalie had to know the person would come after her again—or someone like him—not to mention the law now looking for her.

The woman had to know that her house of cards was about to come crashing down on her at any moment—whether she was guilty or not. Wasn't there still the chance, though, that she wasn't?

As he walked down the hall toward Natalie's room, he noticed the deputy leaning back in his chair outside her door, legs outstretched. The deputy appeared to be asleep. As he got closer, he saw that the man's hat was pulled down low over his eyes. His heart began to race. Things might be dull on the floor, but there was no way a deputy would fall asleep on the job.

He rushed to him, touched his shoulder. The deputy keeled over onto the floor. Brick felt his chest constrict as the man's hat fell away and he saw the blood and the large goose egg on the deputy's forehead. He quickly checked the man's pulse in his neck—strong—before rushing into Natalie Berkshire's room.

Just as he'd known, the bed was empty. He swore. Hadn't he known she wasn't catatonic? Just as he'd known that she'd spoken to Mo. He quickly looked around. The bathroom door was closed. "Natalie?" He stepped to the door and grabbed the knob. "Natalie?" No answer.

He opened the door. Of course the room was empty.

Because Natalie Berkshire was gone.

He started to pull out his phone when he heard a moan coming from somewhere in the room. The sound froze his blood. He wasn't alone in here after all?

Brick spun around. The room was still empty. Another moan. He caught movement under the bed and rushed to push the bed aside. The nurse lay on the floor, gagged and bound with IV tubing. She was attired in nothing but panties and a hospital gown.

As he pulled off the gag and began to untie her, she said, "She jumped me. She took my uniform, my bra, my socks and shoes. She..." The nurse began to cry. "She threatened me. Said if I made a sound..."

"How long ago did she leave?" Brick asked as he freed her.

"Five minutes, maybe more."

At the sound of the deputy regaining consciousness out in the hall, Brick rushed out. "Take care of the nurse and call this in."

"The nurse?" The deputy touched the bump on his head gingerly. His eyes widened as if he realized at last what had happened. "The patient. Is she...?"

"Gone."

"I don't know what happened."

"Say that to my father," Brick called as he ran down the hall.

He told himself that the woman might not have gotten out of the building yet. She was wearing scrubs—just like every other nurse.

Brick took the stairs three at a time and burst out on the lower floor to race for the front door. After pushing out through it, he stopped to glance around the parking lot. He didn't see her.

At the growl of a motorcycle, he spun around and saw a woman in scrubs roar past. Her hair was a dark wave behind her as Natalie Berkshire sailed away.

Brick ran to his pickup and went after her. But he hadn't gone two blocks when he realized he'd lost her. He called it in, but didn't hold out any hope that she would be caught. The dispatcher told him that a young man who'd been in the hospital parking lot was calling to say that a nurse had shoved him off his motorcycle and taken it.

Brick pulled over, slamming his fist down on the wheel. Natalie was in the wind. What were their chances that they could find her? At the moment, she wasn't wanted by the law for anything but questioning. Her life was in danger, though, and she had to know that. Without money or transportation other than a stolen motorcycle, where would she go? Her car had been impounded. And considering what was found in her car, she'd already been running scared before she was abducted. What would she do now?

His cell phone rang.

"I get only one call so don't make me waste it." He recognized the voice at once, a little sultry, definitely direct. "I just heard the news here at the jail," Mo said. "Natalie has taken off. I suspected she'd pull something like this. But I can help you find her if we hurry."

He scoffed. "Too bad you're behind bars."

"Listen," Mo said. "I *know* this woman. I knew she would run when she was released from jail. I knew she'd take off the way she has. You'll never find her without my help. You want the blood of her next victim on your hands? Give it some thought. Then get me out of here." She hung up.

Brick shook his head as he disconnected. He was on a forced medical leave and she was suspended. Neither of them had any authority to go after Natalie. Mo really thought he would spring her?

He knew she'd be out by morning, once she went before a judge. But at least for the moment she was locked up. Unfortunately, that didn't make Natalie safe. Who knew who all was after the woman?

He sat in his pickup for a moment, his mind a rabbit warren of thoughts. What if Mo was right? What if the real person in danger was Natalie's next client?

Starting the pickup, he drove to his apartment. On the way, he half expected to see Natalie in his neighborhood. He knew it wasn't logical. Just as he knew he would always be expecting to see her somewhere until she turned up again. If she ever did. He still hadn't decided if she was a victim or a possible serial killer.

Mo Mortensen thought she knew, but she was too personally involved. He couldn't trust her judgment any more than his own.

At his apartment, he walked in, closing the door behind him. He stood just inside looking around the studio apartment as if seeing it for the first time. Nothing about the space reflected him in any way. It was as if no one lived here. Clearly, it was a hiding place, not a home.

He sighed as he pulled off his Stetson and raked a hand through his hair. His father was right. He wasn't healed. Nor did he have any idea how to put himself back together again. He felt unsure of everything—except the steady beat of his heart. He was alive. He'd survived a bullet. Maybe he could survive the rest. Maybe. But not here in this colorless, empty apartment.

Brick walked over to the wardrobe, pulled it open and began to dump what he might need into a backpack. Swinging it over his shoulder, he took one last look around before he walked out.

Chapter Six

"Took you long enough," Mo said as she held on to the bars of her cell as if trying to bend them. "We've lost valuable time."

Brick shook his head. "You were that sure I was coming for you?" he asked as he held up the keys that would free her.

She smiled in answer, and if he hadn't realized that this woman might be trouble, he was beginning to. "Well?" she demanded. "Did you come to taunt me or get me out where we can find Natalie before it's too late?"

"I'm not unlocking your cell until you tell me what she said to you and why you reacted the way you did." He could see the internal battle going on inside her. For a moment, he thought she would simply move away from the bars, go sit on her bunk, tell him to go to hell. He wouldn't have been surprised.

Except for one thing. She was desperate to find Natalie. He had to know why. He no longer thought it was to harm her. But then again, he could be wrong about that, too. He could be letting another kind of monster free.

"Tell me why her words hit you so hard," he said, and when she didn't answer, he said, "Fine, then stay where you are. I'll find Natalie on my own."

"You won't," she snapped as he started to turn away. "I know how she thinks. You, on the other hand, are convinced that she is some innocent, helpless creature who needs you." She reminded him that Natalie had played him after he'd tried to help her.

"Okay," he conceded, keeping his back to her. "Maybe she wasn't as traumatized as she appeared."

"*You think?* You'd better hope we find her before whoever held her captive does. I'm betting he's also looking for her and will try to abduct her again. You need me."

He smiled to himself as he turned back to her. "And you need me. So…"

"She said Tricia didn't kill herself."

He felt the weight of words fall on him. *What the—?* "What does that mean?"

"Natalie was probably lying. Trying to save her own skin. But if there is a chance she was telling the truth…"

Brick shook his head. "That explains why you looked so shocked. You must have thought there was more than a chance she was telling the truth. But if so—"

"Then someone killed her."

"Why would someone kill your sister?"

"That's what I have to find out. So, are you going

to help me or not?" Mo let go of the bars and met his gaze. "I'll tell you everything. Just get me out of here so I can find her—before someone else gets to her."

Her last words shook him more than he wanted to admit. Natalie had already been abducted and held captive. He didn't doubt that there were others who were determined to see that the woman paid for what they believed she'd done. Mo had been one of them, he knew. Had a few words from Natalie really changed that?

"*We* find her." He waited for her to agree. "We do this together or you stay where you are. I posted your bond. I keep my investment safe by not letting you out of my sight."

"Fine." She motioned impatiently for him to unlock the cell.

He hoped he wasn't making a huge mistake as he inserted the key. "I already picked up your belongings."

"My car?"

"You won't be needing it. My truck's outside," he said as he turned the cell door key.

"My car would be more comfortable, not to mention, I'm an ace driver."

"I'm sure you are. That's why I can just see you leaving me high and dry."

"Have you always been so suspicious?" she asked as they headed out of the building.

"Apparently, since I spotted you for the fake you were quickly enough at the hospital."

She rolled her eyes as they walked together toward

the parking lot. "I thought I made a pretty believable nurse." Her gaze locked with his for a moment. "Until I had to kick your butt."

He laughed. "Yes, there is that score to settle yet."

"Until next time."

"Only next time I'll see you coming."

She chuckled. "Just keep telling yourself that," she said over her shoulder as she continued down the sidewalk.

"MAUREEN?"

They were almost to the parking lot when she turned to see the man who'd called her name coming down the sidewalk toward her. She was as shocked to see her brother-in-law here as he sounded to see her.

"It *is* you," Thomas said as he reached her and Brick. "I saw you coming out of the jail..." His gaze sharpened. "What are you doing in Big Sky?"

"I could ask you the same thing," Mo said, taken off guard by seeing him here of all places. Since her sister's funeral, she'd been avoiding him and felt guilty about it. But Thomas reminded her of all Tricia's hopes and dreams now gone forever. He'd also made it clear that he wanted to put Natalie and the rest behind him, something she couldn't do. "What are you doing here?"

He raised an eyebrow. "I'm here on business. Life does go on, Maureen. But it seems you know that. You're back at work?" He shot a glance at the law enforcement building. He thought she was here also working—certainly not just being released from jail.

She didn't answer as she looked past him to the cute brunette with him. Her eyes narrowed.

Following her gaze, he turned and drew the young woman into the conversation. "This is Quinn Pierson. We work together." He sounded defensive.

Mo instantly regretted making him feel that way. Thomas had been through enough with the loss of his son and wife. Surely she didn't resent that he was here on business with a colleague, probably attending some seminar since she knew that many of them were held here at the resort each year. But she did resent that he'd gone on with his life when she couldn't.

"I'm sorry," she said, meaning it. She saw that he was staring at Brick with the same questioning look she'd given the brunette. "This is Brick Savage. A…friend."

Thomas seemed to turn the name over in his mouth as if trying to place it. Brick's name was unusual enough that she knew he was bound to eventually tie it to Natalie since the deputy's name had been in all the news as the man who'd rescued the distraught woman in the middle of the night. Once Thomas did figure out who Brick was, he'd know what she was up to. Unless he'd already heard about Natalie being in the hospital here before making her daring escape.

But now he merely lifted a brow at her before he stuck out his hand to shake Brick's. "I'm also a friend of Mo's," he said, making her feel worse, if that was possible. He'd made his position clear after the funeral, the last time they'd talked.

"I really don't care what happens to Natalie Berkshire," he'd said. "I never want to hear her name again."

"You don't want justice?" Mo had demanded.

"Justice? My son is dead, my wife is dead. Tracking down Natalie won't bring either of them back."

"But she'll kill again, she'll destroy other families, she'll—"

"I can't do anything about that."

"Well, I can," Mo had snapped. "And I will."

Thomas had begun to cry. "Please, for my sake, if not your own, let it go, Maureen. I can't bear anymore. I'm begging you. Let your sister and the rest of us find some peace."

Had he found that peace? She sure hadn't.

"We really should get going," Quinn said, dragging Mo back from the past. "We're already running late for the seminar." She gave Mo an apologetic shrug and held out a flyer. "I don't know if you're familiar with Palmer's seminars. They're enlightening."

Mo took the sheet of paper without looking at it.

"It was nice to meet you," Quinn said. She really was pretty. And young. The word *fresh* came to mind.

"You, too," Mo said automatically as she wished she hadn't run into them now of all times. As the two walked away, she saw Thomas turn to Quinn and say something. The brunette's soft laugh filtered back, making Mo uncomfortable. She thought about Tricia. Something had been wrong in that house. Natalie had tried to tell her, but Mo hadn't wanted to hear. Now she regretted it.

"You going to tell me what that was about?" Brick said once the two were out of earshot.

"That was my brother-in-law." She realized she hadn't introduced Thomas by his last name. "Thomas Colton. Tricia's husband."

Brick had to catch up to her since she'd turned and taken off, wanting to put that entire scene behind her. Sometimes she spoke before she thought. Change that to *often*. It got her into trouble. She wouldn't be suspended right now if she were capable of keeping her mouth shut.

"He knew Natalie well, I'm assuming?" Brick said as he caught up to her and motioned to where his pickup was parked. She nodded and slowed, no longer cringing, but glad to have put distance between her and Thomas and his…associate.

Once in his pickup, he reminded her that she hadn't finished her story.

She realized she was still holding the flyer the woman had given her. Wadding it up, she tossed it on the floor. "Drive and I'll tell you everything. Natalie already has a huge head start."

He hesitated, but only a moment before he started the truck. "We need to establish some ground rules," he said as he pulled away from the jail. "We do this together. You take off, you go back behind bars. You help me find her, but then she's going to be returned for questioning about her abduction and any other deaths under her employ. Is that understood?"

"Whatever you say."

"I'm out on a limb here. Don't saw it off, because I don't want to be hunting you next."

"We don't have time to argue," she said, dismissing his concerns. "Tell me how she got out of the hospital."

He told her about Natalie taking the nurse's clothing and leaving her gagged and bound half-naked under the bed before stealing a motorcycle and escaping. "She probably got the idea from you."

Mo seemed to ignore that. "She'll be looking for different clothing first. Which way did she go when she left the hospital?" He told her. "Then take that street."

"There are no stores that way."

"She has no money. She'll be looking for clothing she can steal."

BRICK WONDERED IF she was talking about what she would do under the same circumstances—or about Natalie. But he didn't argue. He drove through the residential area as Mo craned her neck down each side street they passed.

"So," he said. "Tell me."

She sighed. Clearly, it was a story she'd condensed, having lived with it for so long. "I stopped by Tricia's that day. She was sleeping so I didn't want to disturb her. She'd been struggling with everything—postpartum depression, the baby's health issues, who knows what else? Anyway, I decided to just look in on Joey. I was worried about him because of all his medical problems and even more worried for Tricia. She'd had trouble conceiving. It looked like she and Thomas weren't going to be able to have children, something Tricia had wanted desperately. Then, out of the blue, she'd gotten pregnant. I'd expected her to be over-the-moon happy, but she seemed anxious all the time. Then, when Joey was born with all the medical problems and the doctors said he probably wouldn't make a year..." Her voice trailed off for a moment.

"That day I sensed something being...off. Joey was fine. He was such a beautiful baby. If you didn't know about his health problems... As I started to leave, Natalie stopped me by the front door. She was trying to tell me something when Tricia came down the stairs. I could tell Natalie was upset. I knew she was worried about Tricia. I was, too."

Brick thought about this for a moment, seeing how upset Mo had become just retelling it. "Natalie never told you what she had to talk to you about?"

Mo shook her head. "We never spoke after that. Natalie was arrested, and evidence was coming out about her. Even if she told me what might have been going on in that house."

"What do you mean, about what was going on in that house?"

Mo looked away for a moment.

"I realize this is hard for you—"

"Thomas and Tricia were my family. I hate talking about personal details of their lives. I hate that because of what happened, their personal lives have become media fodder."

"They were having problems," he guessed. "I would imagine the stress..."

She nodded, some of her anger visibly evaporating. "I think it might have been more than the pregnancy and even Joey's health."

"You don't think Thomas and the nanny were—"

"Having an affair?" She shook her head adamantly. "But something was wrong. Tricia wouldn't talk about it and neither would Thomas—not that I tried very hard. I was so intent on proving Natalie guilty and getting justice that I wasn't there for my sister when she needed me the most."

"That's why you want to believe that she didn't kill herself," he said. "Could there have been another man?"

Mo hesitated a little too long. "She and Thomas had been together since college. They were the perfect couple." As if sensing his skepticism, she said, "He idolized her. He was so excited about the baby. He was a wonderful father."

Brick kept driving, wondering what he'd gotten himself into, when she cried, "Stop! Down there."

Backing up, he drove down the side street until she told him to stop again. By then she was out of the truck. He swore, threw the pickup into Park and went after her, thinking she was already breaking their deal.

Instead, she rushed over to an older house with a long three-wire clothesline behind it. The day's wash flapped noisily on the line except for the spaces where it appeared someone had removed items randomly.

A woman came out of the house brandishing a broom. “Don’t even think about it. What is this, some kind of scavenger hunt?” she demanded. “You’re not taking any more of my clothing.”

Brick quickly introduced himself. “We’re looking for the woman who stole the clothes off your line. Was she dressed like a nurse?”

The woman nodded. “I couldn’t imagine why a nurse would be stealing my clothes.”

“Can you tell me what she took?” Mo asked. “And describe the items?”

The woman lowered her broom and thought about it for a moment. “A pair of my black active pants, my favorite flowered shirt, a pair of jeans and my husband’s hooded sweatshirt. It’s navy. The flowered shirt is mostly red.”

“Thank you. Did you see her leave? What she was driving? Which way did she go?”

The homeowner shook her head. “I saw her taking the clothes and ran outside but she disappeared around the side of the house. Wait. I did hear what sounded like a motorcycle engine. Does that help?”

Brick nodded. “It does, thanks. How long ago was that?”

“Thirty minutes ago, maybe longer.”

“We’ll do our best to get your clothes back for you,” he said and turned toward the pickup.

They were back in the pickup when Mo said,

"She'll ditch those clothes as soon as she gets some money. I hope that woman doesn't hold her breath about getting them back. She'll dump the motorcycle first—if she hasn't already. She'll be looking for a vehicle. One that won't be missed for a while."

Brick shot a look at Mo as he started the truck. "You make her sound like a hardened criminal. What if she's innocent and now has people chasing her who want to do more than hurt her? Maybe she's just trying to stay alive as best she can."

"That's exactly what she's trying to do. She's running for her life."

Brick's cell phone rang. He thought it would be his father. He'd already ignored three calls from him. Instead, it was the deputy from the hospital.

"I heard you're looking for the patient that got away," the deputy said. "I hope you find her. The marshal wants to have my head over this." He explained that while he was getting examined for the wound on his head, he heard that an attendant's purse had gone missing about the same time that Natalie took off. "She thinks the patient who escaped took it."

Brick told Mo.

"Ask how much money was in the purse," she said.

He did and hung up. "Just over a hundred and fifty dollars."

"So Natalie has some money. Now all she needs are wheels," Mo said. "If I were her, I'd be looking around bars, cafés, places where everyday people work and don't worry about their vehicles being stolen."

"Anyone ever mention that you think like a criminal?"

Mo smiled. "Thanks. There's a bar up ahead. Pull in."

As Brick did, his cell phone rang again. This time it was his father.

HUD STARTED TO leave another voice mail on his son's phone when, to his surprise, Brick answered. He'd come back to the office to find out that not only had Natalie Berkshire taken off before the Billings homicide detectives arrived, but his son had broken suspended homicide detective Mo Mortensen out of jail.

"What the hell are you doing?" he demanded the moment his son answered the call. "You spring a woman you don't know from Adam. A woman who is in our jail because she attacked you? Are you trying to end your career before it even starts?"

"I'm on leave, remember."

The marshal swore. "What is that noise in the background?"

"I'm standing outside a bar waiting for Mo."

Hud wanted to scream. "Mo, is it now? Brick..." He let out an angry breath. "I hope the bar doesn't have a back door. Why did you bust her out of jail?"

"She's going to help me find Natalie."

"Are you crazy? You said this woman wants to kill Natalie."

"Maybe she wants to, but she won't. And even if she still did, I won't let her."

He swore under his breath. "Do I have to tell you again that Natalie Berkshire isn't wanted for anything other than questioning at this point? Or that you don't have the authority to go after her, let alone arrest her, even if there was a warrant out for her? Worse, Natalie might not be the woman you have to fear. You could be with the real criminal right now. How do you know she wasn't involved with Natalie Berkshire's abduction?"

"She wasn't. Which means that she isn't the only one on this woman's trail. We need to find her first. I was right about what happened at the hospital. Natalie did say something to her, just as I thought I heard. She said that Tricia, Mo's sister, didn't kill herself."

"What?"

"Apparently there was more going on with that family than anyone—other than Natalie, who lived in the house—knew. If Tricia didn't kill herself, if Natalie didn't take that baby's life, then who did?"

"Brick," his father snapped. "What are you going to do with her if you find Natalie? Maybe more to the point, what is Mo going to do? Even if you find Natalie, you can't restrain her in any way or you'll find yourself behind bars for kidnapping. Clearly the woman was well enough to escape the hospital. Letting the cop who's chasing her out of jail is just asking for trouble."

"Maybe Natalie lied about all of it. But what if she didn't?" Hud heard the music in the background change. Then his son said, "I think I see the motorcycle she stole. I have to go."

He swore as Brick disconnected. He tried to call him back, but the phone went straight to voice mail. He debated putting a BOLO out on both his son and Mo. Natalie already had one out on her. Along with being wanted for questioning, she was wanted for tying up a nurse and stealing a motorcycle and a purse at the hospital. Also at this point, Hud had no doubt that the woman would be safer behind bars.

The marshal looked up to find a deputy standing in his doorway. "Anything more on the motor home?"

"So far I haven't found any that have been returned in the past twenty-four hours that might have been damaged as if someone had broken out of it," the deputy said, clearly unhappy with this assignment.

Hud waved him away, saying, "Keep trying." As the deputy left, he wondered if it wasn't a waste of manpower. Maybe whoever had rented the motor home would be smart enough not to turn it in anywhere nearby. That was if he was right and there'd been damage to it when Natalie had escaped.

HERBERT LEE REINER could feel sweat running down the middle of his back. He watched the two men in the glassed-in vacation rental vehicle office. Whatever they were discussing, it looked serious.

He thought about walking out. The car rental agency was just down the road. He could get there quickly enough. But it would mean leaving behind his reimbursement check. His deposit was a hefty amount—even after the repair bill had come out of it.

He glanced toward the motor home sitting where he'd parked it, then back at the men in the RV rental office. It was hot in here. He wanted to push back the sleeves on his shirt, but then the scratches would show. The clerk, a young man named Gil, had been suspicious enough when he'd seen the damage done to the door in the motor home's one bedroom. Now Gil was in the office talking to his older boss.

His throat dry as dust, Herb spotted the drinking fountain off to the side and walked over nonchalantly, hoping he looked like a man without a care in the world. He turned it on and took a long drink even though the water wasn't quite cold enough. It also had a funny taste. But at his age, everything was either tasteless or strange. Aging taste buds, though, were the least of his worries right now.

Glancing at his watch, he felt time running out. As he took another drink and straightened, Gil came out of the glass enclosure holding his paperwork. Herb felt his heart drop as he saw that the man's boss was now on the phone.

"I really need to get going," Herb said. "Is there a problem?"

"No," the clerk said a little too quickly. "I'm just new at this and I want to do it right."

He tried not to be impatient as he watched the clerk tap at his computer keys. Had Gil been told to stall Herb until the police arrived?

Glancing toward the outside door, he considered making a run for it. But his legs felt as if they'd turned to blocks of wood. He hadn't run anywhere in years and there was his bad knee to consider. He shifted on his feet, looked down and frowned. There was a spot of blood on his right sneaker. The sight elevated his heart rate. He felt his chest tighten.

"I think I have it now," Gil said. The printer began to grind out more paperwork. How much paperwork did it take to un-rent a motor home anyway?

Gil moved to the printer, pulled out the papers and began sorting through them. Through the glass window into the office, Herb saw that the boss was off the phone and looking in his direction.

But the man's gaze dropped the moment it connected with Herb's. His heart was pounding now, making breathing more difficult. If he didn't get out of here—

Gil handed him a stack of papers. On the top was a check for both his deposit and his refund since he was turning the motor home in earlier than he planned. He signed where Gil pointed and picked everything up with trembling fingers.

"Thank you," he said automatically and turned toward the door, trying not to rush.

"I thought you needed a ride?" Gil called after him. "If you can wait just a few minutes—"

He couldn't wait. He burst out the door, expecting to hear sirens in the distance. Breathing in the fresh, cool air, he turned left and began walking toward the car rental agency.

All of the rental places were along a frontage road not far from the airport. He kept walking, checking behind him every few minutes. He was limping a little, the bad knee, as he listened for the crunch of gravel behind him. He was that sure that a patrol car would be pulling up any minute.

He'd thought he was being so smart renting the motor home. But he'd seen Gil's expression when he'd seen evidence of the violence that had destroyed the bedroom door. Fortunately, Gil hadn't noticed where the duct tape had taken the paint off the bed frame.

At the car rental agency, Herb stopped and looked behind him. Cars whizzed past. No cop cars. He hurriedly stepped inside, closing the door, and took a deep breath, trying to quiet his pounding pulse. At this place at least the air conditioning was working, he thought as he moved to the counter.

Had he cleaned up any evidence he might have left in the motor home? That was the question that nagged at him as he again filled out paperwork and produced a credit card and Arizona driver's license.

It wasn't that he worried about being caught. He knew that was going to happen soon enough. He just couldn't get caught until he'd fulfilled his promise to his wife of fifty-two years.

The paperwork took just enough time that he was sweating profusely even in the air-conditioned building. But eventually, he walked out with the keys to a white panel van. The clerk had asked him if he was moving.

"Getting rid of a few things," he'd said.

Once behind the wheel, he drove down the highway to the small coffee shop where he'd left his wife. Dorie was sitting by the window, staring down into her coffee cup as he pulled up. He hit the horn twice. For a moment he thought she hadn't heard.

Then slowly, she raised her head. He figured the sun was glinting off the windshield because it took her a minute to recognize him before she smiled. He was used to her slack-jawed empty stare. Just as he was her confused frowns. Often it was hard to get her attention.

While those times felt like a knife to his chest after all these years together, it was her gentle, sweet smile that was his undoing. In that smile he saw the accumulation of both her pain and his. Their loss was so great they no longer cared what happened to either of them.

Dorie rose slowly from the table inside the coffee shop. As she lifted her head, she changed before his eyes. He saw the young woman she'd been the first time he'd seen her. She didn't look frail. She didn't look like a woman who was dying. He knew all that was keeping her alive was the promise he'd made her.

A part of him had thought Dorie might not be strong enough to go on. He'd told her he would go alone, but she'd insisted that like him, she would see this through. Dorie climbed into the van without looking at him. Instead, she noticed something on her sleeve. As if sleepwalking, she picked a long, dark hair off her sweater and held it up to study it for a moment, her face grim, before she whirred down her window and threw it away.

Finally, she turned to him. “Can you find her again?”

He nodded, knowing that he would go to the ends of the earth for this woman he’d spent the better part of his life with. “I’ll find her.”

Dorie reached over and placed her small, age-spotted hand on his arm for a moment before she looked toward the mountains, that distant stare returning to her beautiful eyes as she absently ran her fingers down the sleeve of her sweater as if looking for another strand of Natalie Berkshire’s dark hair.

Chapter Seven

The light was dim inside the bar. At this hour, the place was packed. Mo stood just inside the door, letting her eyes adjust as she did a quick scan for Natalie. She didn't see her. Behind her, Brick came into the bar, closing the door and the afternoon out. "There's a motorcycle beside the bar. It looks like the one she stole from the hospital parking lot."

Mo nodded. "I'll check the restroom. If you see her—"

"Don't worry, I won't let her get away."

Mo headed for the ladies' room, the smell of beer and nachos seeming to follow her. Her stomach growled and she realized she couldn't remember the last time she'd had something to eat. Brick had broken her out of jail before she'd been fed.

Pushing open the bathroom door, she saw two women at the sinks. One was putting on lipstick, the other drying her hands and talking a mile a minute about some guy she'd met at the bar. Three of the stalls' doors stood open. Two were closed.

As Mo started toward the closed doors, one came

open and a dark-haired woman stepped out in a red shirt. For a split second, Mo thought it was Natalie, but then the woman turned. She moved past and took the stall next to the one with the closed door.

Bending down, she glanced under the neighboring stall. No nurse's Crocs, but that didn't mean that Natalie hadn't changed into the fairly new-looking sneakers in the stall next door. She'd had plenty of time to find a change of footwear.

Mo sat down on the toilet fully clothed and waited. The talkative woman at the sink left with her friend. She could hear water running, then the grind of the paper towel machine. The bathroom door made a whooshing sound and the room fell silent.

Next to her, the woman in the stall hadn't moved. Hadn't reached for toilet paper, hadn't flushed. Mo knew she could be wasting valuable time. Natalie could have already stolen a car from the bar lot and was now miles from here.

She cleared her voice. "I'm sorry, but could you hand me some paper?" she asked the woman in the next stall. "I'm all out over here."

Without a word, the woman pulled off some paper and handed it under the side of the stall. Mo saw the freshly painted fingernails as she took the rolled up paper. Nothing like the chipped ones she'd seen on Natalie's hands in the hospital.

"Thanks," she said, dropped it into the toilet and flushed before she pushed open her door. She was washing her hands when the woman came out of the stall and swore.

Mo saw her looking around. "Lose something?"

"My purse. I left it right there." She shook her head, exasperated. "I hope my friend picked it up for me."

"Any chance you had your car keys in it?" Mo asked. The woman's eyes widened in answer.

As they walked out of the bathroom, she told Brick what had happened. He stepped outside with the woman who'd lost her purse—and her car, as it turned out. He called it in to the marshal's department.

Mo was considering getting a drink while she waited for Brick to return when a male voice said, "Bartender, give that woman a beer on me." She turned in surprise as she recognized the voice.

"Shane, what are you doing here?"

Shane Danby laughed. "Same thing you are, I would imagine. Thought we had come to take Natalie Berkshire back to Billings. But got here too late. The nurse nanny got away. You wouldn't know anything about that, would you? Maybe it had something to do with you being on the wrong side of the law?"

His laugh told her that he knew about her being arrested. "Sorry, but I'm not interested in discussing it with you."

"Not interested in discussing it with me?" he mocked, his voice rough with anger. "You always thought you were better than the rest of us, didn't you, Mo? Well, you aren't the only one looking for Natalie. There's a bounty on her head. That's right, some father of a kid she killed is offering a reward to anyone who brings her in—dead or alive. Everyone in four states is looking to collect. If I find her first I'm going to shoot and ask questions later."

Mo feared it might be true. "And what if she's innocent?" she demanded. She realized that she was starting to sound like Brick. But she couldn't bear the thought that some trigger-happy lawman killed Natalie before she could get to the truth when it hadn't been that long ago that she'd thought that was exactly what she'd wanted. "She deserves a trial."

Shane scoffed. "The crazy psycho deserves the same treatment she gave those patients under her care."

"No wonder you didn't make Homicide." She started past him, but he grabbed her arm and dragged her into an alcove away from the people at the bar. When she started to fight back, he grabbed her by the throat and shoved her against the wall, holding her there with his body.

"Assault, Shane?" she asked around the pain in her throat. "I'm still a homicide cop."

"Are you? That's not what I hear. I heard you went after Berkshire to put her down like a mad dog. Now I'm wondering if you're trying to help her slip the noose."

Just the reminder of how her sister had died brought up a low growl from her throat. "I suggest you let me go."

"Oh, really? Is that what you would suggest?" he said with a laugh. "I can tell you'd like to kick my ass right now." He was so close she could see the dark spots among the brown in his eyes and smell the onions he'd had on his burger for lunch. "The only reason you got Homicide over me is because you're a woman. Gotta meet their quotas." He turned his head to spit on the floor. His hand on her throat tightened. "It's all bullsh—"

The rest of his words were lost as he was grabbed from behind and slammed into the wall next to her. Brick had several inches in height on Shane and was in better shape. He grabbed him by the throat—just as Shane had held her.

"I'm the law, you idiot!" Shane cried and swore.

"You're not the only one," Brick said. "Deputy Marshal Brick Savage. You think you're tough, being rough with a woman?"

As much as she wouldn't mind seeing Brick kick his butt, she stepped in. "Let him go. Trust me, he isn't worth it."

Brick let go of him so quickly, Shane stumbled and almost fell. As Brick started to turn away, Shane picked up an empty bottle someone had left in the alcove and went for him—just as Mo knew he would. She put her foot out, and the lowlife cop went sprawling. The bottle shattered in his hand. As he started to get up, Brick stepped on his hand, pressing it to the glass-strewn floor and making him cry out.

"We done here?" Brick said, lifting his boot to free the cop's bleeding hand.

"Need a man to fight your battles, Mo?" Shane yelled as he sat back to cradle his cut hand.

She stepped around the corner to grab a rag off

the bar and tossed it to him. "Shane, you just don't learn." As she started to turn, he kicked out, catching her in the shin. She spun on him and kicked back, catching him in the thigh. He doubled over, writhing on the floor. "Don't ever grab me by the throat again or next time, it won't be my boot toe. It will be a bullet."

"That man is dangerous," Brick said as they walked away. "From what I heard, he has a grudge against you."

"Shane has a grudge against the world. You can't take him seriously."

"Mo, you need to watch your back around him."

She couldn't help being touched by his concern. "While I appreciate you coming to my rescue, now you have to watch your back as well when it comes to him."

"You could have taken him." He was studying her as they walked.

Mo nodded. "I could have that time because I saw him coming. That's the problem with men like Shane Danby. When he's most dangerous is when you don't see him coming. But he told me something disturbing." Mo told him about the bounty. "It might be a lie. But it also might be true, in which case we have to find Natalie before anyone else does."

"WELL, AT LEAST WE know what Natalie is driving," Brick said as they left the bar. A deputy from the department was taking down the information on the stolen car. He and Mo hadn't needed to hang around to listen to the description of the thief the woman from the car was giving the deputy. "There's a BOLO out on the car. I wouldn't be surprised if she's picked up within the hour."

Mo snorted as she and Brick left. "Have you ever noticed how large Montana is?" She shook her head. "There isn't enough law enforcement to cover it all. But more important, Natalie grew up here. She knows the state. She'll know where to go."

He glanced over at her. "You really have no faith at all in the law, do you?"

Mo was busy calling up a map on her phone. "If you wanted to go to the closest small town, which one would you chose?"

"West Yellowstone. Or cut across to Ennis. They're both small. She'd be harder to find in Bozeman, though."

"Ennis," she said emphatically. "Let's go."

Ennis wouldn't have been his choice, but he didn't argue. Mo said she knew Natalie. He headed south down the canyon toward the cut-across to Madison Valley and Ennis. "I'm curious. How did your sister find Natalie?"

"Through the hospital. Natalie had left her information there. She had a great résumé. She seemed perfect since she specialized in patients with special needs and she'd worked as a nurse nanny."

"Did your sister get references on her?"

Mo nodded. "She made a few calls, but once she met Natalie, she liked her so much she didn't bother checking the rest of the references."

Brick thought of the woman he'd seen on television and photographed in the newspaper. Slightly built, Natalie was a plain, nonthreatening young woman with what he would have thought of as an honest face.

"It was for such a short time since Tricia planned to stay home full-time, but had to tie up loose ends at her job. Also, Natalie didn't mind the short-term employment. Mostly, Tricia was just so grateful to find someone so experienced. But I know a lot of it was that she liked Natalie right away. I did too when I met her. She had this way of making you feel at ease around her. It's no wonder that she's fooled so many people."

"If she's guilty," he said, and she grunted.

As he drove past the turnoff to his family ranch, he glanced in that direction. A cold chill ran up his spine to lift the hair on the nape of his neck. He had the worst feeling that he might not ever see it again. It was a crazy premonition that something bad would happen and he'd never make it home again. He didn't believe in premonitions. He wondered what the shrink he saw would make of it. But it still shook him.

"You know anything about her background?" he asked to clear his own thoughts.

"Trying to profile her? Good luck with that. It's pretty boring. She was raised on a ranch in eastern Montana, two hardworking parents, an only child. She was valedictorian and president of her senior class. Got top grades in nursing school and excelled at the two hospitals where she worked before going into in-home care."

"Was she ever arrested before?" he asked as he drove down the canyon. The sun dropped behind the mountains and twilight began to cast long shadows in the canyon.

"No. Not even for a parking ticket. But who knows about her other nursing jobs? Apparently the patients all had life-threatening medical problems. Most of them weren't expected to live, so when they died..."

"But she was never a suspect before, right?"

"That doesn't mean that she's not guilty," Mo said defensively. "Maybe this time she wasn't as careful. Or the medical examiner was more qualified."

He glanced over at her. "But now any deaths where she was the nurse are in question." He drove in silence as he thought about the woman he'd seen in his headlights not even twenty-four hours before. "I'm sorry, but I keep thinking, what if she really is innocent? We hear about babies dying of SIDS or doctors being unable to pinpoint what caused a death. Maybe she wasn't responsible for any of them. Maybe it's just bad luck on her part. And if what she told you is true..."

"If it's true, why didn't she tell the police?"

"Maybe she did. I doubt they were apt to believe her. You're still not sure you do."

She shot him a look before she said, "Let me know when we reach Ennis or if you need me to drive." Then she turned away from him and a few minutes later, he heard her slow, rhythmic breathing and realized she'd fallen asleep.

Mo came out of the nightmare fighting.

"Whoa! Take it easy," Brick cried as he held up a hand to ward off her blows while keeping the pickup on the road with the other.

She sat up blinking as she fought off the remnants of her bad dream. She could feel Brick's questioning gaze on her. She ignored him. No doubt he'd seen and heard enough as she was coming awake to know it had been a nightmare. She didn't want to talk about it and hoped he wouldn't ask.

Through the pickup's windshield she could see lights ahead illuminating the small Montana town on the horizon. "Ennis?" she asked, sitting up straighter, still trying to shake off the dream. It was a familiar one. Some things changed, but the feeling was always the same. She was trapped in a small, dark space all alone and yet there was someone nearby. She could hear them breathing. Then she heard something rattle. Whoever was out there wasn't content to leave her to die. They were coming in for her.

"Ennis," he said, stealing glances at her. Fortunately, he didn't ask, but she knew he was wondering about her—as he should be. "What now?" he asked as he drove into the tiny Western burg.

"Food and then somewhere to sleep."

That surprised him. "I thought we were in a hurry to catch her."

"We are. If I'm right, she's already here. She won't leave until she is forced to."

He seemed surprised, but only said, "Well, I could

definitely eat something," as he pulled into a space in front of a log cabin café.

But neither of them moved for a moment as if happy not to be in motion after hours on the road.

HERB LICKED HIS praline ice cream before it melted down the cone and watched the couple that had just driven up in the pickup. He recognized the man behind the wheel. Deputy Marshal Brick Savage had been pointed out to him as the man who'd discovered the abducted woman.

"Enjoying your cone, Dorie?"

She smiled over at him, chocolate ice cream on her lips.

They'd gotten ice cream on their very first date fifty-three years ago. He'd known then that he was going to marry her. Their future had been so bright. There'd been a few bumps in the road over the years, but nothing they hadn't been able to overcome together.

Until the death of their youngest grandchild, the first boy out of six. Their daughter had named him Herbert after his grandfather, an honor that had brought tears to Herb's eyes. He'd been so happy and had gladly offered to pay for a full-time nanny to live in the house and help their youngest daughter with her first child, since the baby had some special medical needs.

He wiped at an errant tear and noticed that his ice cream was melting. He quickly turned his attention back to his cone—and the pickup. The occupants hadn't gotten out. He could see the woman sitting on the passenger side. Another cop? The hospital had been in pandemonium over what had turned out to be a suspended homicide detective pretending to be a nurse, he'd heard when he'd stopped by. The woman had gotten into Natalie Berkshire's room—right past the deputy stationed outside the door.

Herb wondered what the cop had been planning to do. Or if she was merely trying to find out who had taken Natalie captive. That was when he'd decided it was time to get rid of the motor home.

Seeing the two law officers here in Ennis, he knew he'd been right about where he could find Natalie again. He realized that they might be able to help him. He glanced over at Dorie. She'd almost finished her cone. She looked content for the moment and that alone made him happy.

Unlike him, he thought she had moments when she didn't remember what had happened to their only grandson. What a blessing for her and one that he just assumed he wouldn't have until he died, which wasn't that far off given the way he'd been feeling lately.

But first, he intended to take the woman who'd killed his grandson with him as soon as he found her again. It was time.

HUD WALKED INTO the old two-story house on Cardwell Ranch, hung his Stetson on the hook by the door and dropped onto the bench to take off his boots.

"You look exhausted," Dana said as she hurried

to help him with his boots, an offer she'd given him most nights since they'd married. Tonight, though, he seemed glad for her help as if he needed it badly. For months, she'd been encouraging him to retire. Their children were raised, and she suspected it wouldn't be that long before they had grandchildren.

"It was one of those days," the marshal admitted as he gave her a wan smile. "You're going to hear about it soon enough anyway..." He seemed to brace himself. "Brick..." He raked his fingers through his graying hair.

Sometimes it hit her how much they'd both aged. Like now. Normally when she looked at her husband, she saw the young, big strong man he'd been when she'd fallen in love with him. She was still desperately in love with this man, looking past the gray and the wrinkles and the slight stoop of his broad shoulders.

"Brick has gotten himself involved in a case that could blow up in all of our faces," Hud said finally.

"I thought he was technically still on medical leave?"

"Tell that to him. I told him until I got the release from the head doctor..." He met her gaze. "He's still having the nightmares, I know he is. He thinks he's fine. You know him."

"Is this about the woman he found?"

Hud nodded. "She escaped from the hospital after taking a nurse's clothing and leaving the woman tied up under the bed."

Dana gasped. "This is the same woman that someone had abducted and held?" He nodded. "Why would she do something like that?"

"I suppose she's scared. Or she heard Billings homicide was on its way to question her. But what complicates it is this cop who's after her..."

"The one who attacked our son?"

For a moment, he looked surprised that she'd heard that detail through the grapevine. He shouldn't have been. He had to know how talk moved down this canyon.

Hud sighed. "We had her behind bars, but Brick broke her out. Now the two of them have gone after the woman who escaped the hospital. Brick to save her and...who knows what Mo has planned."

"Mo?"

"Maureen 'Mo' Mortensen, the suspended cop who your son is now mixed up with."

Dana had to bite her tongue. She'd been against Brick going into law enforcement from the beginning. For years she'd worried about Hud's safety every time he left the house to go to work. She didn't want to have to worry about one of her sons, as well.

"He was born to do this," her husband said as if seeing her expression. She met his gaze, too upset to speak. "I didn't encourage him. And I certainly didn't approve of this. But you know how he is."

"He wants to please you," she said, her voice breaking. "He idolizes you, so of course he wants to follow in your footsteps." Hud said nothing. Clearly he had to know there wasn't much he could say. She saw how difficult this was for him. He was worried and upset. She felt her anger vanish as quickly as it had appeared.

Stepping to him, she wrapped her arms around him. He pulled her down on his lap and buried his face into her neck. "Brick will be fine," she whispered. "He's enough like you, he'll be fine."

Hud nodded against her shoulder, and she tightened her arms around him as she hoped it was true. His cell phone rang, making her groan. That was another reason she was anxious for him to retire. They deserved peace and quiet at this age—not the constant sound of a phone ringing at all hours and Hud having to go take care of marshal business.

She stepped from his arms so he could take the call. But she didn't go far. If this was about Brick… She listened to her husband's side of it, something about a motor home being found. So *not* about Brick.

Turning away, she headed toward the kitchen to bake something, anything. That was what she did when she was upset—bake. She didn't want to know about the dark things her husband dealt with daily. She didn't want to think about what Brick had involved himself in or how dangerous it might be.

She turned on the oven, anxious to smell something sweet filling up the old ranch house kitchen.

"I CAN'T BELIEVE Natalie would stop this soon," Brick said as he looked around at the busy main street as people were enjoying the warm summer night. Everywhere there were tourists with their campers and sunburned kids, fishermen wearing fly vests, an older couple sitting outside eating ice cream cones and watching all the activity. "But I can see where she could blend in here since the locals seem to be outnumbered."

His comment rated him one of Mo's smiles. This one actually reached her blue eyes. He felt himself grow warm under the glow of it and warned himself to be careful. If she turned it on him too much, he might find himself feeling close to her and that would be a mistake, especially given his reputation—and hers.

"Natalie knows this area. She went to college in Bozeman so she's floated the Madison River on tubes, drunk beer in Bogert Park's old band shell and sledded Pete's Hill. There are just some things you do when you attend Montana State University. Or at least we did back in the day."

He turned toward her. "You went to MSU?" She nodded. "Did you know—"

"Natalie?" She shook her head. "But we were there about the same time. I wouldn't be surprised if we crossed paths and didn't know it." She seemed to be studying the activity on the main street.

He followed her gaze to all the people dressed in shorts and sandals. It made him think of a summer when his parents took them to Yellowstone Park. Growing up on the ranch, there was no such thing as a lazy summer. There was always work to do. It was why he used to sneak away and find a place in the shade to take a nap, but his mother always found him. She would scold him and before she was through, she'd suggest they all go down to the creek for a swim.

That summer in Yellowstone he'd felt like one of the tourists. It had been a great summer with his twin, Angus, brother Hank, sister Mary and cousins Ella and Ford. He realized Mo was staring at him.

"Nice memory?" she asked. "Let me guess. There's a girl involved."

He laughed. "As a matter of fact, there is. My mother." He told her what he'd been thinking about and the picnic lunch they'd had in Yellowstone, swimming in the Firehole, watching Old Faithful go off at sunset before pitching tents at Lake Campground and sitting around a campfire roasting marshmallows. Ranch kids often didn't get those kinds of trips. Too many animals that needed tending to. "The whole trip was my mother's idea."

She didn't say anything for a moment. "She sounds like a great lady."

He smiled. "She is. Not that Dana Cardwell Savage isn't tough when she has to be. She's one strong, determined woman." He met Mo's gaze. "A lot like you."

"She doesn't want you doing this, does she."

Brick leaned back behind the wheel, watching tourists stream past for a moment. "She doesn't want me doing a lot of things, including becoming a deputy marshal."

He could feel Mo openly studying him. "Maybe you should listen to her."

He turned so he was facing her. “You don’t think I have what it takes?”

“I didn’t say that.”

“But it’s what you were thinking.”

She shook her head. “Don’t assume you know what I’m thinking.” They both grew quiet. “I just don’t want to be responsible for your mother having to attend your funeral.”

“Then you’d better make sure nothing happens to me,” he said and laughed. “Look, it’s nice to know you care, but I’m not your responsibility. This is my choice and I can take care of myself.”

He followed her gaze. Mo was watching the older couple down the street. They were taking all day to eat their ice cream cones. “And you aren’t responsible for me. If the only reason you’re here is to stop me, well, I just hate to see you risking your life for nothing.”

“What was your nightmare about?” he asked.

“I don’t remember.” She opened her door. “I thought you said you were hungry?”

Brick knew a nightmare when he saw one. He found himself watching Mo out of the corner of his eye as they took a booth inside the café.

After the waitress brought them menus and water, he opened his, but found himself distracted by what had happened in the pickup earlier. Mo had been sleeping soundly when she began whimpering. He’d asked if she was all right, but hadn’t gotten an answer. Her whimpering had become louder and stronger and she began to quiver until he'd reached over and touched her arm.

She'd come unglued, swinging her fists at him, her blank blue eyes filled with terror. Did this have something to do with Natalie and her fears that the woman was telling the truth and Tricia didn't take her own life? Or was there more about Maureen Mortensen that he had to worry about?

"I'll take the special, the chicken-fried steak," Mo was saying. "Mashed, white gravy and the salad with blue cheese."

He hadn't realized that the waitress had come back until Mo spoke. He closed his menu. "I'll take the same." He could feel her staring at him.

"I wish you wouldn't," she said, when the waitress had picked up the menus and moved away.

"Wouldn't order what you did?"

She mugged a face. "Wouldn't ask."

He nodded sagely. "Wouldn't ask about your nightmare. I'm guessing it isn't your first. I say that because I've had a few of my own lately."

Mo seemed surprised to hear that.

Brick looked away. "Supposedly I almost died after being shot. But I don't think that's what's causing the nightmares. I killed a man after he shot me."

"Your first." It wasn't a question. She picked up her fork and her napkin and began to polish the tines.

"What about you? Have you had to kill someone as a cop?"

She put down the fork and picked up the knife

and began polishing it. "Why did you order the same thing I did?"

The woman was anything but subtle when it came to changing the subject. "I wasn't paying any attention to what was on the menu. I was more concerned about you."

"Having doubts about coming with me now because I had a bad dream?"

He shook his head. "I had doubts about going anywhere with you long before that." Their gazes met across the expanse of the table and held for a long moment. He felt heat race along his veins.

The waitress put down their salads, breaking their connection. Mo laid her knife down and picked up her fork again. He watched her eat her salad, wondering if she'd felt that flutter at heart level that he had just moments ago. The waitress brought the rest of their food and Mo dug in, avoiding his gaze. He was hungry too and happy to just eat in the companionable silence that fell between them.

"You're a cowboy, right?" she asked halfway through the meal. "So why follow your dad into law enforcement?"

"I grew up on Cardwell Ranch, yes. But I never wanted to just be a rancher." He shrugged. "When I heard that a deputy marshal position was opening up, I thought, why not? I found out that I could do a lot of my year at the police academy online. The rest I'll do once I get my medical release." He looked up and met her blue eyes and again felt as if he was falling down a deep well before she shifted her gaze back to her plate. "When Natalie stumbled out into the street in front of my pickup that night..." He shook his head. "The more I learned about this case, the more I wanted to know what happened."

"You want to solve it."

"Don't you?"

She shrugged and continued eating for a moment. "Law enforcement isn't for everyone. It can be dangerous and soul-stealing. It can take you to places you never wanted to go and can never forget." She looked up, locking eyes with him. "It can change you into a person you no longer recognize."

"Was it law enforcement that did that? Or Natalie Berkshire?"

Mo said nothing as she finished her meal. But her words were still haunting him as they left the café. As they climbed into the pickup to drive to the closest motel, he saw her freeze for a moment.

"What's wrong?" He followed her gaze up the street.

"Nothing. I thought I saw... Never mind. I just imagined it. Let's go."

But he noticed how quiet she was as they checked into a room with two beds. Had she thought she'd seen Natalie? Or someone else?

"And yes, I got us just one room *because* I don't trust you, in case you're wondering," he said as she looked at the two queen beds that took up most of the space.

"If I wanted to get away from you, I could."

"So why haven't you?"

She seemed to study him. "I either like your company or I think you might come in handy."

He raised a brow. "Let's be clear. I'm here to keep you from doing anything stupid when we find Natalie."

Mo smiled as she closed the distance between them. "I asked around the jail about you. I know about your reputation with women. You're a heartbreaker."

He started to object, but she placed a finger against his lips to silence him.

"You won't be breaking my heart, and please don't take that as a challenge." She had a great smile. Her lips turned up at one corner a little more than the other. It was cute. She was more than cute. She was adorable, but also dangerous if the pounding of his heart was any indication.

He pulled her finger from his lips. "Like I said—"

"Right, you're just here to protect Natalie and me from myself." She moved within a breath of her lips touching his lips. "Then I should be able to rest peacefully tonight knowing you will keep me from doing anything…stupid."

As she stepped away, he let out the breath he hadn't realized he'd been holding.

EARLY THE NEXT MORNING, Hud looked up from his desk to see his deputy standing in front of him, grinning. "You found the motor home we're looking for."

"Well," he said, his grin shrinking some. "I think

so. It was returned yesterday, and it did have damage to one of the bedroom doors."

The marshal got to his feet. "Tell me it hasn't been cleaned or the damage repaired."

"It hasn't. It was rented by a man named Herbert Lee Reiner out of Sun Daisy, Arizona."

Arizona? Hud recalled one of the inquiries he'd gotten about Natalie Berkshire was from Arizona. "Send a forensic team." He frowned. If the man had used his real name to rent the motor home, then maybe this wasn't the right one.

As the deputy left his office to notify the team, the marshal returned to his computer to gather what information he could about Herbert Lee Reiner. Married to Doris Sue Thompson for fifty-two years. Herbert had been a postman until his retirement. That meant his fingerprints would be on file.

It didn't take long before their names began coming up in newspaper articles. The articles read much like the ones that had run in the Billings newspaper. The older couple were the grandparents of an infant with health problems born to their youngest child. The other name that came up in the baby's death was Natalie Berkshire.

BRICK WOKE TO the sound of the shower. He looked around the motel room, then at the queen-sized bed he lay in. The covers weren't overly disturbed. He hadn't had a nightmare. That alone surprised him.

He stretched, feeling better than he had in weeks. That too surprised him. Maybe what he'd told his father was true. Maybe this was exactly what he'd needed, something he could sink his teeth into, he thought as Mo came out of the bathroom in nothing but a towel.

"Oh, good you're awake." She dug in her suitcase, pulled out jeans, a T-shirt and white panties and bra. "I thought you might want a shower," she said pointedly when he hadn't moved.

He'd been doing his best not to look at her since the towel was pretty skimpy. "You think I need one?"

"I just don't want to have to try to dress in that dinky bathroom." She cocked her head toward the open bathroom door. "Do you mind?"

He threw back the covers and swung his legs over the side. Last night he'd slept in his boxers and nothing else. He hesitated.

"I've seen men in a lot less," Mo said, shaking her head with obvious amusement.

As he strutted past her into the bathroom, he heard her chuckle. He stepped into the bathroom and opened his palm to remove the keys to the pickup he'd grabbed before coming in here. He tucked them under a towel and turned on the shower, smiling to himself. If Mo was planning to leave in his pickup this morning, she was in for a surprise.

He recalled last night when she'd told him he wasn't going to break her heart. It had sounded way too much like a challenge, he thought. But that was the old Brick. He hadn't been serious about any woman—at least not for long. That apparently was how he'd gotten the reputation—news to him.

When he thought about Mo, about the look they'd shared at the café, about how his body had reacted with her standing so close last night and again this morning in that towel… The woman had been taunting him. Well, if she thought for a moment that he was going to make a move on her…

Brick turned the shower to cold for a few moments before climbing out. He wasn't going to let this woman distract him. In the mirror, he ran his fingers through his dark hair. It was a lot longer than he usually wore it, he thought. Also, he had a day's stubble. He rubbed his jaw, but decided to leave it, not wanting to take the time to shave. Grabbing a towel, he dried off, then pulled on his boxers. He stepped back out of the bathroom.

Mo was gone.

Chapter Eight

Mo looked up as she came out of the local grocery store. From the expression on Brick's handsome face, he'd thought she'd left him for good. She could see that he was upset and trying to hide it—now that he'd found her. She felt almost guilty for giving him a scare. Also for giving him a hard time last night. She had seen firsthand that the man definitely had a way with women. But then, she'd known that the moment she'd laid eyes on him.

He was too good-looking, too cocky, too full of himself, she'd told herself. And yet since they'd hooked up, so to speak, she'd seen another, more vulnerable side of him. Not that she was going to let that fact weaken her resolve to keep everything between them professional.

"You could have left a note," he said, walking up to her.

She laughed. "You sound like we're a thing. If you must know, I went out to get us some doughnuts and coffee," she said, indicating the bag she was holding in one hand and the to-go tray with two coffees in the other. She handed him the bag, then took one of the coffee cups from the tray and handed it to him. "Also, I looked for an apartment." He blinked. "Not for us, sweetie. For Natalie."

The morning was sunny and just starting to warm up. She could smell pine and river scents drifting on the breeze. There was a picnic table on the lawn in front of the small motel. She walked to it and sat down. To anyone watching, they might look like a married couple on vacation.

She opened the bag of doughnuts and offered one to Brick as he joined her.

He took a glazed one and said, "An apartment for Natalie?"

"If you were her, what would you do? She can't keep running. We know she has limited funds. She has to look for a job. Why not a small tourist town where people with money have built huge summer homes and would love a nanny? Most are probably from out of state and have never heard of Natalie Berkshire—not that she will use her real name, I would imagine. It would only be for the summer or maybe just a few weeks. Exactly what she's looking for."

He shook his head. "I'm still surprised she'd stop so close to where she was caught."

"Because she knows that we expect her to run farther," Mo said and took a sip of her coffee. "She needs to find a job, and if I'm right, disappear into a family with her next victim. She's getting desperate. I believe that's why she made the mistake she did."

"What mistake was that?" he asked and took a bite of his doughnut, chasing it with a sip of coffee. He frowned at the cup in his hand.

"You do take your coffee with sugar and cream, right?" she asked.

He looked up in surprise. "How did you—"

"It's no mystery. You had an old cup in your pickup. It was written on the side along with your name and the logo of your favorite coffee shop." She grinned.

"Okay, you're observant. I'll give you that. What mistake did Natalie make?"

"She let her guard down and got caught. She'll want to do what comes naturally to her, which isn't running. She's here in this town. I feel it." Mo saw his skepticism and reached into her pocket to take out a scrap of paper. She handed it to him. "The apartment comes with a garage where she can hide the stolen car—if she hasn't had a chance to get rid of it already."

"Where did you get this?" he asked as he turned the strip of paper over in his fingers. He had nice hands, she noticed. Long fingers. Strong, tanned hands. A man's hands. She felt a shiver at even the thought of those hands exploring her body.

"You want my jacket?" Brick asked, thinking she was chilly. He was already starting to take off his jean jacket.

She shook her head. "It was on a bulletin board in the only grocery store in town advertising a studio apartment cheap with the telephone number on the slips of paper on the bottom. Only one other slip of paper had been pulled off so I figured the ad hasn't been posted for long."

"That doesn't mean Natalie took the other one."

She nodded in agreement. "But there is one way to find out." She pulled out her phone and called the number. No answer. She left a message saying that she was looking for a long-term rental and hoped the apartment was still available.

When she looked up at Brick, she expected to see disapproval in his expression because of how easily the lie had come to her lips. Instead, he was rising to his feet, his eyes fixed on his pickup parked in front of their motel unit. She watched him walk over to the truck and pull what appeared to be a folded sheet of paper from under the passenger-side windshield wiper.

As he unfolded the paper and read what was written there, his gaze shot to her. Mo felt her heart begin to pound.

BRICK HANDED Mo the note he'd found on his pickup's windshield. He watched her quickly unfolded it and read the words neatly printed there.

> Chasing me won't give you the answers you want. You should be looking for the man Tricia had been seeing. I don't know his name. I only saw him once. Blond with blue eyes, about six-two or six-three. I swear I didn't hurt the baby.

But if Joey was her lover's baby… By the way, someone is following you.

He watched her refold the note and put it into her pocket without a word. He could tell that she was upset, but what was written on the note didn't seem to come as a shock compared to what Natalie had already told her at the hospital. Was it why she hadn't let Natalie tell her that day at the house before Joey died? She hadn't wanted to hear it, still didn't want to believe it.

"We going to discuss this?" he asked when she still said nothing.

Mo opened her mouth, but closed it as her cell phone rang. She checked the phone and then took the call, listening for a few moments before she said, "That's too bad. I'm one of the new teacher aides at the elementary school." Brick's eyebrows shot up. The woman was a born liar. "Do you have any other units?" If Mo were right, Natalie would have only taken the apartment short-term, apparently now making the landlord regret renting it. "I'm moving here soon and anxious to get settled into a place." Again she listened before she smiled. "I'd love to see it." If Natalie had rented the apartment, she would have already been moved in, he thought.

Mo gave the man her number again and disconnected. "He's going to call the new renter to see if she's home and he can show the apartment. She only rented it for a few weeks." When the phone rang, he started and saw Mo take a breath before she picked up. "Hello? Yes? Oh, that's too bad. But could you at least tell me where it is? I could drive by. If I like the area, I'll get something temporary until it opens up."

He saw her nod before she disconnected. "Let's go," she said and started for her side of the pickup. "She's at the apartment. But the call from her landlord will probably spook her."

"You're that sure the woman who rented the apartment is Natalie?" he said, wondering if Mo was ever wrong about anything. She didn't bother to answer, her gaze on the street ahead as she repeated the directions to the apartment that the landlord had given her.

Brick felt his pulse jump. This could be it. They could be about to confront Natalie. Ennis was already busy, the traffic slow and congested until they got away from the main street in town. He tried to remain calm, uncertain how this would go down. He could see Mo tapping the edge of her side window with her fingertips, clearly impatient. Clearly anxious. He was glad he was driving instead of her. She wore an expression that told him she would have plowed through the cars and pedestrians, horn blaring.

The apartment was in an older area of town. He drove down the street slowly, looking for the stolen silver SUV in a state that had hundreds of silver SUVs.

"The apartment is on the third floor, a small one-bedroom with stairs off the back," Mo said. "That's it." She pointed at a tall white building with navy trim that had clearly once been a single dwelling, now made into three apartments. Two bikes were chained to the front porch. A small pickup was parked out front along with a smaller compact car next to the two-car garage.

He pulled over. "I don't see a silver SUV, but I suppose it could be in the garage."

"She probably ditched it and picked up something else." Mo opened her door, climbed out and started across the street.

"We're taking her back to Big Sky for questioning," he reminded Mo.

"You wouldn't have found her if it hadn't been for me," she said under her breath as they approached the apartment house. "You'd be looking as far away as Spokane."

"Mo—"

"I just need to talk to her, so let's find her before we debate what to do with her."

He knew she was right. It felt as if they were chasing a ghost. He glanced behind them, thinking about the note. Was someone really following them? Look how easily Natalie had found them. He remembered Mo thinking she saw someone last night. Natalie? If so, the woman had seen them and could have followed them to the motel.

"I'll take the back stairs," Mo said now. "You go in the front door. Bleeding heart or not, try to remember that this woman is dangerous." She took off at a run around the back.

He headed for the front door, determined to get

to the woman before Mo did—if Natalie was in this building. Brick tried the front door, not surprised when it opened into a small foyer. There were two doors and stairs.

He took the stairs two at a time, no longer worrying about making too much noise. If Natalie had rented this apartment, if she was still up there…he had to get to her and fast.

At the top of the stairs, he found a door and quickly stepped to it to knock. He thought he heard a sound on the other side of the door and for a moment, he thought about drawing his weapon. Mo had warned him that Natalie was dangerous. But he remembered the terrified woman he'd seen in his headlights. The woman lying in the hospital bed. He still wanted to believe that she was a victim, an innocent victim. He left his gun holstered and tried the door.

It opened, startling him.

"Come in," Mo said on the other side of the doorstep. "She's gone."

"Natalie?" Mo didn't answer as she turned back into the apartment. He followed, a little stunned. Had she been right about Natalie renting this place? "How do you know for certain it was her?"

She shoved a copy of a local shopper at him. It was folded so that the want ads were on top. Several positions had been circled. His heart slammed against his ribs as he saw they were for nanny positions. One of them for an infant that needed special care.

Mo had moved into the bedroom, where she was standing at the end of the unmade bed.

"Are you all right?" he asked her. She wasn't moving, hardly appeared to be breathing. He realized that his heart was still thundering in his chest. Mo hadn't just been right about the apartment. She'd been right about Natalie looking for another job. A possible new victim.

"Maybe she'll come back," he said.

Mo shook her head. "She's gone. I found something interesting in her trash in the bathroom. She's changed her appearance, cut her hair and colored it red." He could hear regret in her voice. They'd come so close. They couldn't have missed her by more than a few minutes.

Her gaze met his, but only for an instant as she pushed past him and left.

He stood for a moment looking at the room. From what he could see, it appeared that the renter had left in a hurry. One of the drawers in the bureau stood open and empty. The door to the small closet was open, the metal hangers bare. That was if Natalie had even had time to pick up more clothing. He suspected she was traveling light.

They'd gotten close. Just not close enough.

He found Mo outside, leaning against the side of his pickup. She appeared to be looking up at the snowcapped mountains. But as he drew closer, he saw that her eyes were closed, her chest heaving as if she was having trouble breathing.

As he approached her, her eyes opened. A lock

of blond hair fell over one blue eye as she turned to him abruptly. "You still think she's innocent?" She sounded angry and upset and disappointed, he realized. Disappointed not just because they hadn't caught up to Natalie. He had a feeling she was even more disappointed in herself for not wanting to hear what Natalie had tried to tell her that day at the house.

"You can't second-guess yourself," he said quietly. "You can't change what happened."

She shook her head and looked away. "No, but I can find out what happened to my sister. I can make sure Natalie doesn't hurt anyone else."

Did he still think Natalie was innocent? Did he think the circled job openings were about her needing to get back to work because she needed money? Or as Mo said, a woman looking for her next victim?

He squinted toward the mountains. "I want to find her as much as you do."

Mo shook her head. "You don't. Which is why you need to go back to Big Sky and your job before you lose it. Don't throw your career away like I did. This isn't about you."

"It's about justice. Without it, we're nothing but outlaws. And if I went back, I'd have to take you with me. I'm not sure I can trust you to appear at your hearing."

She met his gaze and held it. "Fine, stay. Just remember, I warned you."

Her cell phone rang. She pulled it out of her pocket and looked at the screen before she stepped away to take the call.

MO HEARD THE anger in Thomas's voice and groaned inwardly. "That man you were with the other day," her brother-in-law said without preamble. "Deputy Marshal Brick Savage? He's the one who found Natalie—and lost her again. Maureen, what are you doing?"

She realized it always bothered her that he'd never called her by her nickname. It had always been Maureen. "Thomas, why have you never called me Mo?"

"What?"

"I just realized that you've never called me by my nickname."

"Are you drunk? Or have you just completely lost your mind?"

"Thomas—"

"What are you doing, *Mo*?" He sounded more pained than angry now. "I begged you at the funeral to let it go. Joey is gone. Tricia is gone. Why are you destroying your life, too? I called the police station. They said you've been suspended. Please, Maureen, Mo, whatever. *Stop.*" His voice broke.

She felt a painful tug at her heart. She'd met Thomas at college when her only eighteen months older sister had started dating him. They'd hung out with the same crowd. He was like a brother to her. She'd been maid of honor at their wedding.

"I can't talk to you about this," she said. "It doesn't have anything to do with you."

"How can you say that?" he asked, raising his voice. "Joey was my son, Tricia was my wife. Natalie was like a member of our family. This has been a nightmare. One I just want to put behind me."

"I wish I could, but I can't."

"So, what are you going to do?" he demanded.

She looked back at Brick leaning against his pickup, waiting for her. They needed go after Natalie. She was getting away. Again. She thought about telling Thomas about the note, about Natalie saying that Tricia hadn't taken her own life, but didn't. Like he said, he was trying to put it all behind him. Until she had even a shred of proof that it was true, she needed to keep it to herself. She didn't want to hurt him any more than she already had. "I don't know what I'm doing." She could almost see him shaking his head.

"The cops let her go, Maureen."

"That doesn't mean she was innocent."

"But it could, couldn't it?" He sounded as if he was pleading. "Isn't it possible Joey just died? The doctor had said he might die. If he'd lived, he was going to have to have all those surgeries and even then, the doctor said he might never…" His voice broke again. She could hear him crying.

She'd done this. "I'm so sorry. This is why I didn't want to tell you."

"Then don't do this. Go back to work. It's the only thing I've found that helps. I'm sure you can get back on at your old job if you leave all of this behind. You know you being obsessed over this is the last thing Tricia would want."

She didn't know what to say because she knew

it was true. But then again, she questioned if she'd ever known her sister at all. Tricia was having an affair? It seemed impossible. She still didn't believe it, but knew she had to find out the truth no matter where it led her.

"You and I shouldn't have any secrets, Maureen. We're..." His voice broke again. "Family."

Her heart clinched. The worst thing about this was lying to Thomas. His losses were so much greater than hers. And now she had him worrying about her.

"I need you to be all right," he'd told her at Tricia's funeral. "I can't bear losing anyone else."

The anguish in his voice now broke her heart all over again. "I'll be okay," she said, wondering if it would ever be true. She'd told herself that she would be fine as soon as she got the justice her sister and Thomas deserved. But she wasn't even sure of that anymore.

"I know I can't stop you, but promise me this. That you'll call every few days, Maureen. I need to hear your voice. I need to know that you're okay."

"I'll call," she said. "Thomas?" She searched for something to say that would help them both. "It's going to get better." At least she hoped so.

Chapter Nine

“Your brother-in-law?” Brick asked as Mo pocketed her phone and walked toward him and his pickup. She nodded without looking at him. “You all right?”

He watched her look away to hide her raw emotions. “You don’t have to worry about me.”

“I wish that were true.” When she met his gaze, he reached over to brush a lock of her hair back from her face. “You’re having second thoughts.”

She shook her head. “You have no idea what I’m thinking.”

“I see more than you think. You’re conflicted about all of this.”

“Of course I am,” she snapped and tried to step past him, but he blocked her way. She sighed. “What is it you want me to say? That maybe you’re right and I’m wrong? Don’t you think I wish that were true?”

“What if it is?”

She glared at him, clearly losing her patience. “Here is the problem. When we find her, and we will, you’ll still be debating it all in your mind. She will use that against you and you’ll end up dead.”

"You've made her into a monster with powers that don't exist."

She scoffed at that. "This woman's greatest advantage is that she doesn't look or act the part. It's her strongest defense and most dangerous attribute." She pulled out the folded note he'd found on his pickup's windshield. "You think I don't want to find out if this is true? You think I don't want to believe that my sister didn't take her own life?"

"Why would Natalie lie?" Brick asked.

"It's nothing but a distraction. So instead of going after Natalie, I chase my sister's death only to find out it was all a lie. But by then, Natalie is long gone. She's living in someone else's house, taking care of a patient for a family who has no idea what horror has walked through their door." She pushed past him. "We need to get moving."

MO FELT CLOSE to tears. She couldn't help being upset. She hated hurting Thomas more than he was already suffering. Add that to her disappointment. They'd come so close to catching Natalie. She could feel the note in her pocket, the words burned into her brain. Tricia was having an affair. She didn't want to believe it. Just as she didn't want to believe any of this was happening.

And yet, it was happening. It had happened. What if Tricia really did have another man in her life? Did that really change anything? Unless it was true and Tricia hadn't taken her own life. All Mo could think was, why hadn't she known? She and Tricia used to be so close. How had she not known what was going on with her own sister?

"Where to now?" Brick asked as they climbed into the pickup cab again and he started the engine.

She pulled out her phone to call up a map and tried to get her emotions under control. Thomas's phone call had gutted her. She kept thinking of the wedding. Her sister had been so happy. The two had been in love since college. Everyone said they made the perfect couple. But after trying so many times to have a child and failing… Is that when everything changed?

"Take 287 north," she said to Brick and pocketed her phone. "We'll watch the truck stops, the convenience stores." In truth, she had no idea what Natalie would do now. "She'll be wanting to get rid of the vehicle she's driving."

"While you were on the phone, I spoke to one of the neighbors. He said she left in a hurry, driving a tan older model two-wheel-drive pickup, so she's already dumped the car she stole in Big Sky," Brick said.

She looked over at him. "Nice work."

"This one sounds like it might have been cheap enough that she bought it with the money she's stolen so far."

Mo nodded. "I suspect Natalie's been living on the run for a long time, afraid to stay anywhere for too long. She's at the point now that she'll do whatever she has to do to survive." A part of Mo felt that way, as well. She'd given up everything—her job, the life she'd made for herself, her savings—to find this woman.

What am I doing? Chasing a possible killer and if so, when and how would it end? She feared the answer.

FROM DOWN THE STREET, private investigator Jim Cameron slid down behind the wheel as he watched the two climb into the pickup. He held the phone tighter to his ear.

"I'm looking at them as we speak," he said into the phone. "The female cop and the deputy marshal."

"Did they find Natalie?"

"No. Apparently she went out the back before I got here."

"Stay on it. This has to end."

He thought about the elderly couple that had cruised by in a sedan earlier—before the cop and the deputy had arrived. He'd noticed the way they'd stared at the three-story house.

"There's this old couple," Jim said. "I've seen them too many times and they drove by, both of them staring at the house."

"I'm not worried about some old couple. Stay on the cop and the deputy. Make sure they don't find Natalie first."

Jim shook his head. As many people as there appeared to be after this woman, himself included, none of them had gotten their hands on her except for whoever had abducted her in Big Sky. And the woman in question had managed to escape.

"Keep me informed." The line went dead.

Jim disconnected and sat up a little. The cop and the deputy had been sitting in his pickup unmoving so far. This had seemed like a simple enough job when he'd taken it on. If he wasn't getting paid so well…

He tried not to question what exactly was going on. It seemed to him that Natalie Berkshire was doing her best to crawl into a hole and stay there. Why roust her out? Why keep forcing her to run? Why not let her land somewhere and then throw a net over her?

The pickup with the cop and deputy was moving again. He waited a few moments before he fell in behind it.

BRICK DROVE THROUGH the residential area toward the center of town. Mo was lost in her own thoughts. What would Natalie do now? Run! What choice did she have? This time, she might run farther and be harder to find.

They were almost to the main drag in town when Mo saw the lights of police cars and what appeared to be a wreck in the middle of the intersection. As they drew closer, an officer waved him around the two-vehicle accident. She saw that a sedan had been involved—and a tan older model two-wheel-drive pickup.

"Isn't that the couple we saw eating the ice cream cones last evening?" Mo asked as he started to drive past the couple the police were talking with.

"Maybe, but that definitely looks like the description of the pickup Natalie was driving," Brick said.

"Stop." Mo threw her door open and she was out, slamming it behind her. She heard the cop order Brick to keep moving as she disappeared into the crowd gathered at the scene.

"Did you see what happened?" she asked several people on the street.

"That older couple T-boned that pickup with the woman inside," a man told her. "I swear that elderly driver sped up just before they collided."

"What happened to the woman in the pickup?" Mo asked. From where she stood, she could see that the driver's side of the pickup was caved in—and the passenger door was hanging open.

"She got out of the passenger side and limped off before the cops arrived," a woman said. "She was hurt, bleeding, but she took off down that way. The police are looking for her. Maybe she thought the accident was her fault and she wanted to get away. Or she was so shaken up that she didn't even know what she was doing."

"How badly hurt was she?" Mo asked.

"She was limping," one of the bystanders told her. "And bleeding."

"I bet she doesn't get far," someone said.

Mo wouldn't have taken that bet.

She continued down the street until she spotted Brick. He'd pulled over into the first parking space he'd found and now stood next to his truck, waiting. That he knew she'd find him made her realize how much their relationship had changed. Only this morning he'd thought she had taken off. She didn't know what had changed or when—just that it had. Smiling to herself, she realized she was actually glad to see him and had to swallow the lump in her throat as she joined him and told him what she'd learned.

AS BRICK CLIMBED behind the wheel, he pulled out his phone. "There's something I want to check." He called his father's cell. The marshal answered on the first ring. "Brick—"

"Before you start in, didn't you tell me that the woman at the convenience store said the man in the motor home was elderly?" He knew he'd hit on something when all he heard for a moment was silence.

"We found the motor home," his father said. "A forensic team found evidence that it was the one where Natalie Berkshire was held captive."

"And the elderly driver?"

"Herbert Lee Reiner and his wife, Doris Sue, out of Sun Daisy, Arizona. They're grandparents of a woman whose baby died. Natalie was the nanny. I have a BOLO out on them."

Brick felt his stomach drop as his father described the two. "They just tried to kill Natalie in Ennis. She's on the run again, although injured after her vehicle was rammed by their car. I just thought you'd want to know." He disconnected before his father could lecture him and turned to Mo to tell her what he'd learned.

"So we head up Highway 287 north?" he asked

as he started the pickup and glanced in his rearview mirror. He'd seen a dark SUV earlier. But now he saw nothing suspicious.

"Change of plans," Mo said. "What would you do if you'd just lost everything again and were now injured?"

"Go to the hospital?"

"Not just any hospital. You'd go to where your ex-husband the doctor worked. He's a surgeon at the hospital in the state capital—and not that far from here."

Chapter Ten

On the drive to Helena, Mo seemed to relax. He respected how she seemed to bounce back from disappointment quickly.

"Tell me about Brick Savage," she said out of the blue.

He glanced over at her for a moment before turning back to his driving. "Not much to tell," he said, wondering if she was just bored or if she were really interested.

"I doubt that's true since your reputation with women precedes you. Apparently you like to lasso them, but you always set them free."

"I wouldn't believe everything you hear." He cleared his throat. "You want to hear my life story or just the raunchy parts?"

She laughed. "I want to hear it all," she said, settling into her seat for the drive.

"Okay. I was born and raised in the Gallatin Canyon, grew up on a ranch with a mother who ran day-to-day operations and a father who was the local marshal. My whole family lives in that canyon. Ranching and wrangling is all I've ever known."

"And yet you're a deputy marshal," she said. "Or will be if I don't get you fired before you even start."

He ignored that. "I guess in the back of my mind I always thought I would follow in my father's footsteps."

"Will working with me ruin that for you?" she asked, sounding actually concerned.

"Don't worry about me." Brick had to admit, he'd always been impulsive, going with what felt right at the moment. He'd never felt rooted to the ranch the way his siblings had. He'd always been a free spirit.

Then again, he'd always had his twin brother, Angus, the solid, steady one, to help steer him out of trouble—until recently. Not to mention, he'd also had his very wise cousin Ella. But now he was on his own since both of them had moved on with their lives.

And now here he was. On his own. Two rogue lawmen. He couldn't depend on Mo to steer him into anything but trouble.

"So you said you were shot. An angry husband?"

"I've made a habit of steering clear of married women. My brother and I and my cousin Ella were helping a rancher in Wyoming on a cattle drive. Her husband, who she was divorcing, was giving her a hard time. I just got in the way of a bullet."

"That explains a lot. It was all about rescuing a woman in distress. You just can't help yourself, can you?"

He shook his head and sighed as they reached the

Helena hospital where they would find Natalie's ex. "You just like giving me a hard time, don't you?"

Mo grinned. "Now that you mention it…"

THE TALL, DARK-HAIRED doctor came into the room on a gust of air-conditioned breeze. He closed the door and went straight to his desk, sitting down behind it before he considered the two of them. Clearing his voice, he glanced at his watch and asked, "I don't have a lot of time before my next surgery. What is this about?"

"We're here about your ex-wife Natalie," Mo said, trying to see the woman she'd known with this man. In the time she'd spent time around the woman, Natalie had never mentioned her ex.

"Natalie and I are no longer married."

"We are hoping you'd seen her today," Brick said.

Dr. Philip Berkshire shook his head. "Why would I? I haven't even seen her in years." He started to rise.

"She contacted you for bail money when she was arrested," Mo said.

He slowly lowered himself into the chair. "I said I hadn't seen her. I didn't say I hadn't heard from her."

"She didn't call you today?" Brick asked.

"No. She called when she needed bail money, and I turned her down."

"Why?" Brick asked.

"Why?" the doctor seemed shocked by the question. "Because I don't owe her anything."

"Or because you believe she's guilty?" Mo asked.

"The two of you worked together. That's how you met and married, right?"

"That was a long time ago. I know nothing of the kind of woman she is now."

"What kind of nurse was she?" Mo asked.

"She was a fine nurse, a devoted, compassionate nurse."

"Why did she quit nursing to become a nanny?"

"You would have to ask her that."

Brick shifted in his chair. "I would love to, but since she's not here and you are…"

"We divorced."

"Why?"

Berkshire shot Brick a narrowed look. "That's personal."

"Look, we're trying to find her. Her life is in danger," he said. "Also, she might have information that we need in another death."

The doctor closed his eyes and slowly shook his head. "She had this thing about babies, sick babies. I'm sure you already know this," he said, opening his eyes and turning his attention on them again. "She had a younger sister who was born very sick. The doctor had given the infant only weeks to live. Natalie told me that she couldn't bear the child's suffering and was relieved when the baby passed. That is what you're looking for, isn't it? A reason?"

"You think she put her sister out of her pain and suffering?" Mo asked, feeling sick to her stomach. What if it had begun when Natalie was only a child herself?

"I think she wanted to. Whether or not she did… I believe it's why she became a nurse and why when we divorced, she left the hospital to become a nanny for fatally ill children."

"Is she capable of killing a suffering infant?" Brick asked.

Berkshire steepled his fingers in front of him, studying them for a moment before he spoke. "Not without causing herself great harm. If Natalie is anything, it is too caring. She was incapable of keeping any distance between herself and her patients. I could see how it was eroding her objectivity. She was too involved, too compassionate."

"Does she have a close friend that she might turn to?" Mo asked, hoping for some clue where the woman might be headed now that she was injured.

He shook his head and then shrugged. "I have no idea."

Brick leaned forward in his chair. "She was injured in a car accident in Ennis. I thought maybe she might have come to you for help."

"No. Natalie wouldn't come to me. Not after I wouldn't give her the bail money. Her pride wouldn't allow that."

"What about her family?" Mo asked. "Would she go to them?"

"Her mother's dead and she had a falling out years ago with her father when her mother got sick. Look, I'm sorry, but I'm scheduled for a surgery," he said as he rose to leave.

Mo asked for directions to Natalie's father's house

and the doctor told her. "What kind of falling out?" she asked as he headed for the door.

The doctor stopped but didn't turn around. "Her mother asked Natalie to help her die." With that, he was gone.

BRICK FOLLOWED A long dirt road that cut across arid country bare of little more than sagebrush. They'd been driving all day across Montana, from Ennis to Helena and now to the eastern portion of the huge state. He was wondering if they'd taken a wrong road when they came over a rise and he saw an old farmhouse in the distance.

As they grew closer, he could see that the two-story stick-built house was once white. Over the years, the paint had faded and peeled until now it was a windswept gray. The yard resembled other ranch and farmyards he'd seen across Montana. Ancient vehicles rusted in the sun along with every kind of farm implement. An old once-red barn leaned into the breeze. A variety of outbuildings were scattered like seeds over the property.

As they pulled down the driveway, an equally weathered looking man came out the screen door. Shading his eyes, he watched the pickup approach as if he hadn't seen anyone this far out in a very long time.

Brick parked, killed the engine and got out. He heard Mo exit the pickup and wondered what she was thinking as she took in this place. This was where Natalie had grown up?

"You lost?" the man asked. His voice and on closer inspection, his face, though weathered, was closer to fifty than eighty. Brick realized he was probably looking at Natalie's father.

"We're looking for Natalie Berkshire," Mo said.

Before she could get the words out of her mouth, the man was shaking his head. "Never heard of her," he said, already turning back toward the house.

"She's your daughter," Mo snapped.

The man stopped, his back to them. "Not anymore."

"She's on the run from people who want to hurt her," Brick said quickly. "She's injured and scared and probably has no one else to go to. Why wouldn't she come here?"

The man let out a deep-rooted bitter sound and slowly turned to face him. "Because she knows better than to come here."

"You wouldn't help her?" Brick asked, finding it hard to believe that blood wouldn't help blood.

"I wouldn't throw water on her if she was on fire."

"I don't believe that," Mo said.

"What do you know about anything?" the man demanded.

"I know she's your only child and if there is something wrong with her, then you have to share in that blame."

The man narrowed his eyes, anger making his nose flare. "Leave my property before I get my gun and run you off. That girl was a bad seed from birth." His voice broke. "Her mother tried to save her with love and look where that got the woman. Dead and buried." There were tears in his eyes as he went back inside, slamming the screen door behind him.

MO WATCHED THE arid landscape sweep past as they drove back to the two-lane highway. Neither of them had spoken as if they didn't know what to say. As Brick pulled up to the stop sign, he glanced over at her.

"Which way?" he asked.

For a moment, she didn't know how to answer. They could drive to the closest town, where Natalie would have gone to school, find someone who knew her when she was young, maybe even find out why the woman's father hated her so much.

But Mo realized that none of that would help. For all she knew, the car crash could have caused internal bleeding and Natalie could be lying in a ditch somewhere, dying or already dead. Or she could have appropriated another vehicle and stolen some cash, and was on her way to her next job in another city, even in another state.

Mo had to make a choice. She felt as if she was at a crossroads. Maybe Natalie had nowhere to go, no one to help her. If she wasn't badly injured, she would keep going. Maybe Brick was right and it wasn't Mo's job to stop the woman—even if she could.

So what did that leave? Keep chasing Natalie or face a possible truth about her sister? If she wanted answers, she was going to have to find them herself without Natalie's help. A part of her still believed that Natalie was lying. But if she wasn't… It was a chance she couldn't take.

Brick was still waiting. "South to Billings," she said. "If it was true and Tricia was seeing another man, I need to find out who he is and what part he might have contributed to all of this." She kept having nightmares about that day and what role she may have played herself. Maybe if she'd listened to what Natalie had to tell her then…

He turned onto the highway headed south. Mo leaned back in the seat and closed her eyes for a moment. She feared sleep, especially after meeting Natalie's father. If that didn't bring on more nightmares, she didn't know what would.

She could tell that man had shaken Brick, as well. When Natalie told her that she grew up on a ranch, Mo had pictured rail fencing, horses running around a green pasture, a large house with a mother baking in the kitchen. She realized that Natalie had let her picture that, wanting Mo to believe that she was a born and bred Montana girl as open and honest as the big sky.

Victim or monster? Mo still couldn't say. Brick wanted to believe the best. But even if Natalie was the murderer Mo believed she was, it didn't mean that she'd killed Joey. Who was this woman and how much of what she'd told her was true?

"I believe that Natalie knows more than she told the police," she said. "More than she's told me. She was trying to warn me that day. She seemed worried about Joey. Worried…" She looked over at him and felt tears fill her eyes. She was fighting to make sense of all of this.

She looked away as he voiced her worst fear.

"Worried that Tricia might have harmed her own baby?"

Mo quickly wanted to argue that Tricia wouldn't, couldn't. But in truth, given the condition her sister had been in the last time she'd seen her, she didn't have an argument in response. Fortunately, Brick didn't give her a chance.

"Natalie was living in that house, right? Of course she would have seen things, overheard things… If she didn't kill Joey, then someone else with access to that house did. If there was another man…"

Mo felt the weight of his words and hated that he was right. "It's time to find out if anything the woman has told me is the truth." Whether she wanted to hear it or not.

Chapter Eleven

Brick couldn't help but question how far he would go to see this finished as he drove toward Billings. He'd been hell-bent on saving Natalie Berkshire, convinced that she was a victim. He still was determined to see that she got a trial. With all the evidence he feared was coming out against her, a trial, it seemed, would only land her in prison for the rest of her life.

And yet not even Mo was now convinced that she'd hurt Joey. Unless Natalie was lying. Was she lying about everything else, as well?

As he glanced over at Mo, he knew that no matter what, he would see this through. Mo needed him, even if she didn't think so. He smiled to himself at the thought as he listened to the sound of the tires on the highway as the miles swept past. And he had needed her. He felt himself getting stronger. Not just physically but emotionally, as well.

Whatever happened now, he and Mo were in this together. As they crossed high prairie, the sun setting behind the Little Rockies, he kept thinking about

Natalie's ex and her father. Was the young woman a bad seed?

He thought of that old couple that had rammed her pickup and injured her. Guilty or not, she deserved better. He hoped that old couple got the book thrown at them, then remembered what his father had told him. The couple had lost their grandchild and believed Natalie was responsible. Not that it gave them the right to take the law into their own hands.

"So if Natalie is the person you suspect she is, how long do you think she's been doing this?" he asked, realizing that his greatest fear was that Mo was right and Natalie would kill again.

"I wouldn't be surprised to find out that this started a lot longer ago than we know. I'm sure there has always been a lack of evidence. Maybe she wasn't even a suspect in most of the cases. Natalie seems to have the ability to be whatever she thinks other people need. Her father aside, I do believe there is something very wrong with her and that her childhood played a part in making her the woman she is now." Mo looked over at him. "Or maybe she is completely innocent of not just Joey's death but the others that are now being reinvestigated."

"Maybe," he said, though no longer sure of that. He realized that he was tired of thinking about it. Right now he was more interested in the woman sitting in the pickup cab next to him. "What about you?"

"What about me?" she asked, sounding surprised by the question.

"I've told you my life story—"

"Hardly."

"And you haven't told me anything about you."

She shook her head. "You know everything that is of any interest."

He scoffed at that. "So, where did you grow up?"

"Really?" She sighed. "Southern California."

He waited, but of course she wasn't forthcoming with more. "A surfer girl."

She scowled. "What is it you're looking for?"

"Maybe just polite conversation."

She gave him a look that said he'd come to the wrong place for that. But after a moment, she said, "My aunt raised me after my parents divorced and couldn't hold it together long enough to raise a child."

He hadn't been expecting that and he was sure his expression showed it. "What about your sister?"

"She was eighteen months older, so she went to live with our grandmother who said she could use the help." Mo shrugged. "Gram was a sour old woman but Tricia got along with her fine, I guess."

"So how was it living with your aunt?"

"I loved my aunt and uncle. They were wonderful to me. My uncle was from Mexico and they owned an authentic Mexican restaurant. I worked there from the time I was nine. I loved it. In fact, my happiest memories are of hanging out in the kitchen as they cooked. There was always music playing and laughter. My uncle cooked the best mole sauce you have ever tasted." She kissed her fingers. There were tears in her eyes.

"Are they still—"

"They were both killed in a drive-by shooting when I was weeks away from eighteen. Before you ask, yes, it is probably why I studied criminology in college and became a cop. I'd already gotten a scholarship so I headed to the same college where my sister was enrolled, Montana State University. Enough?"

"I'd ask about your love life—"

"But you're way too smart for that," she said. "Stop up here. I need something to eat."

As he pulled into a convenience store on the edge of a very small town, his cell phone rang.

"Want me to get you something?" she asked.

"Surprise me." As she climbed out of the cab, he took the call.

"Where are you?" his father asked without preamble.

He felt his pulse jump. "What's happened?" he asked, hearing something in his father's marshal voice.

"Natalie Berkshire has been found. She's dead. She died of her injuries from the car accident."

The breath he'd been holding came in a whoosh as he watched Mo moving around inside the convenience store. He wondered how this would impact her. He felt shaken.

"Herbert Lee Reiner and his wife Doris have been arrested in Ennis for her abduction and her death."

Brick didn't know what to say. "Maybe if we hadn't gone after her—"

"Son, there have been more investigations being reopened. It appears there were a lot of suspicious injuries and deaths at her past jobs."

"You're telling me that she was guilty."

"She might have seen them as mercy killings."

Brick shook his head. He'd wanted to believe she was a victim. He'd wanted to believe he could save her. Or at least keep her safe until she could have a proper trial. His father was right. He'd gotten too involved. Maybe he wasn't cut out for law enforcement after all.

"It's over. You need to come home."

Brick couldn't speak for a moment as he thought of the night Natalie had stumbled into his headlights and how that had led to this moment and the blonde homicide cop standing at the register inside the convenience store.

"It's not over. Not yet. If Natalie was telling the truth then she wasn't responsible for the baby's death and Mo's sister was murdered."

His father swore. "You have no idea what you're getting yourself into. Even if you don't get killed, you could end up in jail."

"That's a chance I have to take. Mo needs my help."

The marshal swore. "You've always led with your heart instead of your head."

"And that's a bad thing?" he joked as he watched Mo finish paying inside the store.

"Not according to your mother," his father said with a sigh. "I wish you'd come home."

"Pretend I'm up in the mountains camping until you see me again." Mo headed out of the store. "Thanks for letting me know."

"Brick? Promise me you'll be careful. Maybe especially with your heart."

As he disconnected, Mo looked up at him, stopping in midstride as if seeing the news etched on his face.

He got out of the truck and went to her. "That was my father. They found Natalie. She died of her injuries from the car crash. The older couple has been arrested."

Her expression didn't change as she nodded. And then she was in his arms, sobbing against his shoulder. He held her, unsure if her tears were of relief or of grief. Like she'd said, she'd known the woman, she'd liked her. But she'd been terrified that Natalie would kill again if not stopped. Now, though, there was no chance of finding out anything more from Natalie. They were on their own.

As quickly as she'd thrown herself into his arms, Mo stepped out of them and wiped her tears before climbing into the cab of his pickup.

"I'm sorry," he said as he slid behind the wheel, not sure of his own feelings. It wasn't what he wanted for Natalie. He wanted justice, but that might have been years of waiting for numerous trials where she was found guilty. She might have ended up on death row in one of the states or merely spent the rest of her life behind bars. If truly guilty, she might have been saved from all that by dying from her injuries.

"I'll understand if you want to stop this," he said to Mo, realizing that this might change everything.

She'd been sitting, holding a convenience store bag on her lap, and staring out the truck windshield. But now she turned to look at him in surprise. "I can't stop now. I have to know the truth. All of it. But you don't have to—"

"I'm in this with you. All the way."

She smiled through fresh tears for a moment before opening the bag in her lap. "I brought you doughnuts. If you're going to be a cop..."

"So... Billings?" She nodded and handed him a doughnut. He took a bite and shifted into gear.

Several hours later, they were on the outskirts of the largest city in Montana. They approached from the north, giving Brick a different view than he normally had approaching the city. He could see the bands of rock rims that ran on each side of the Yellowstone River—and the city. From this vantage point, higher than the city itself, it appeared to be lush green. The bowl between the rims was a canopy of treetops and a green ribbon of Yellowstone River.

And somewhere in Montana's largest city hopefully were the answers Mo so desperately needed.

EARLIER, MO HAD insisted on driving part of the way, letting Brick sleep. They'd stopped in Roundup at the convenience store to use the restroom and get something more to drink, and Brick had taken the wheel again.

"Where do we start?" he asked now as he drove through what were known as The Heights before dropping down into Billings proper.

"Tricia had a friend from high school and college who she still saw. If anyone knows what might have been going on with my sister it will be Hope."

He shot her a look, hearing something in her tone. “A friend you don’t like.”

She looked over at him in surprise. “It isn’t that I don’t like her—not exactly.” She mugged a face. “Fine, I don’t like her. I never trusted her. I always thought Tricia felt sorry for her. Hope is one of those people who demands a lot of sympathy. I swear she makes her own bad luck just for the attention.”

“You were jealous of her relationship with your sister.”

Mo rolled her eyes but didn’t argue the point since he was right. She gave him directions to the woman’s house. The house was small and located in an older neighborhood that had seen better times. Weeds grew tall in the yard and the siding could have used a coat of paint years ago.

“You think she’s back from work?” he asked as he pulled up out front and checked the time.

Mo snorted. “If she had a job,” and opened her door to get out, but stopped.

BRICK COULD TELL she was about to tell him he didn’t have to come with her. But apparently changed her mind, adding, “On second thought, she’ll take to you right off.”

He wasn’t sure he liked that, but followed her up the walk nonetheless.

The thin, dark-haired woman who answered the door wore a tank top and shorts. Her feet were bare. She had a plain face made plainer by her straight shoulder-length hair.

She frowned at Mo, clearly questioning what she was doing on her doorstep. But when her gaze took him in, she smiled and gave him a more welcoming look.

"I didn't expect to see you," Hope said as she jammed her hands on her hips and glared at Mo. "You weren't exactly friendly at the funeral."

"It was a *funeral*, not a party you were invited to." Brick could tell Mo was wishing she didn't need this woman's help. He thought Mo might want to try sugar rather than vinegar in this instance, but kept his mouth shut.

"Look, Hope, I didn't come here to argue with you about some past slight or misunderstanding," Mo said.

"What? You didn't come by to apologize?"

As if seeing that her tactics weren't working, Mo said, "Hope, could we please come in? I need to ask you something about Tricia."

The woman in the doorway hesitated, her gaze going back and forth from one to the other of them before she stepped back with obvious reluctance.

Once inside, Hope didn't offer them a chair. Instead, she stood just inside the door, arms crossed waiting.

"Thanks, we'd love to sit down," Mo said and walked into the living room to perch on the edge of the couch. She looked at Hope and snapped, "Could you drop the drama queen act? I need to know if Tricia had a lover."

Brick had moved to the fireplace and stood waiting to see how all of this was going to shake out. Hope looked pointedly at him without moving.

"This is Deputy Marshal Brick Savage. He's helping me investigate Joey's death," Mo said.

"Wait, *you're* investigating? I heard you got kicked off the force and aren't a cop anymore."

"I was suspended, not fired. Are you going to answer my question or just give me a hard time?" Mo sounded tired and weary. Brick knew the feeling. It had been another long day.

Hope must have decided to cut Mo some slack because she dropped her belligerent stance and moved away from the door to take a chair at the edge of the living room.

"If Tricia had wanted you to know what was going on in her life, she would have told you," Hope said haughtily.

Mo swore. "Tell me who the man was."

"Tell me why I should? Tricia's dead. I promised her I wouldn't tell anyone ever, especially *you*."

"How long had she been seeing him?"

Hope looked away for a moment. "Over a year."

Brick heard Mo emit a painful sound that made Hope smile. But he knew what Mo had to be thinking. There was the possibility that the baby had been her sister's lover's and not Tricia's husband's—just as Natalie had questioned.

"Was she in love with him?" Mo asked.

Hope shrugged. "At first it was just a fling. She didn't think it would last. I think she realized that she'd gotten married too young and she wanted to see if she'd missed out on something. Apparently she had. It was thrilling, she said. I think it was fun because it was a secret. No one knew but me. Your sister knew what you'd say if she told *you*."

Mo seemed to ignore that. "Did you meet him?" Brick saw the answer. "So you never met him."

"They had to keep it secret. Billings may be the largest city in Montana, but it isn't so large that you can have an affair and people don't find out," Hope said.

"So you don't know his name," Brick said, making the woman look over at him. He got the feeling she'd forgotten all about him until then.

"I didn't need to know his name," Hope said irritably. "But why should I tell you even if I did know?" she demanded of Mo.

"Because I have reason to believe Tricia didn't kill herself."

The woman's eyes widened. *"Seriously?"*

"Seriously."

"So..." Hope was frowning again. "You think someone killed her?" Mo said nothing. "You can't think it was Andy."

"Andy?"

Brick saw that Mo's eyes had widened in surprise. "Who is Andy?" he asked.

"A friend of Thomas's."

MO COULDN'T BELIEVE THIS. "Andy? It's Andy?"

"She never told me it was Andy," Hope said

quickly, backpedaling. "Just that it was someone from college, someone she'd had a crush on."

With relief, she realized that if Natalie had been telling the truth, the man Tricia had been having the affair with was blond and more than six feet tall. Andy was short and dark-haired.

She looked at Hope, wanting to throttle the woman. "So you never saw him, never met him. I'm beginning to wonder if Tricia even confided in you."

"She did!" the woman cried. "She was in love and heartbroken because she didn't want to hurt Thomas."

"She was in *love*?" This wasn't adding up. "I thought it was just a fling?"

"At first. She thought it was just for fun, but then it turned into something else and then..." Hope looked away.

"And then she got pregnant," Mo guessed. All those months of trying to get pregnant with Thomas's child and suddenly she had an affair with another man and got pregnant. "Whose baby was Joey?"

Hope shook her head. "She didn't know. She was in a panic. I tried to get her to take a DNA test before the baby was born."

"Did she?"

The woman shook her head. "She was determined that it was Thomas's. She broke off the affair. She told me her boyfriend was really upset."

Mo thought about the emotional roller coaster Tricia had been on during her pregnancy. No wonder she'd been all over the place. "Did her boyfriend not want the baby?"

"Oh, no, he wanted it. He wanted her to leave Thomas and marry him, but she was having second thoughts, regrets, you know. Thomas had found out that she was pregnant and was so happy that she convinced herself that it was his and lied to her boyfriend about taking the test. She said the baby was her husband's and that the affair was over."

"But she didn't know who Joey's father was?"

Hope shook her head. "Then when he was born with so many medical problems and the doctor said he probably wouldn't live..."

Mo knew her sister. "She blamed herself."

"I told her it was stupid. That it was just bad luck."

Mo sat back on the couch. This explained so much. Natalie must have seen how out of control Tricia had been. Once she saw Tricia with the other man... "If you think of anything she might have said about the man that might give me a clue who he was..."

"Like I said, she didn't tell me that much about him. Mostly she talked about the way he made her feel. He was like her. He loved animals." Mo thought about her sister's disappointment that she couldn't have a dog because Thomas was allergic. "And he was romantic," Hope was saying. "One time he carved their initials into a tree."

Mo pulled out of her thoughts to look at the woman. “Where was this?”

“On a camping trip they took some weekend when Thomas was at one of his seminars. Their inside joke was how taken Thomas was with the Jeffrey Palmer seminars.” She looked over at Brick. “Jeffrey Palmer is a self-made millionaire. He gives leadership seminars that he charges a fortune for so others can believe they might one day be rich, too. Thomas idolizes him and never misses one of his seminars, especially since his company sends him along with his associates so they can become leaders.”

“The carving on the tree,” Mo said pointedly. “Where was it exactly?”

Hope seemed to give it some thought. “I think it was near Red Lodge by a creek.” She shrugged. “I just remember how happy Tricia was.”

“Until she wasn’t.”

“I hope you find him. I do remember that when Tricia told me about breaking up with him over the pregnancy, she didn’t come out and say it, but I could tell that she’d been worried about how he was going to take it. She said he was so angry, she’d never seen him like that, and she was sure that she’d done the right thing by breaking it off, but then later he called. She sat right here and cried her heart out. I think she really loved him.”

Mo felt her heart ache for her sister. “She kept seeing him, didn’t she?” Hope looked away, answer enough. Mo got to her feet, thanked her and started for the door.

Brick asked behind her, “Where was this photo taken?” She turned to see that he was pointing at a snapshot that had been stuck into the edge of a framed photograph on the mantle.

It appeared to be one of Tricia. In the photo, her sister was smiling at the person taking the photo. She did look happy. Behind her was a stream and pines.

“Oh, I forgot all about that photo,” Hope cried. “Tricia left it here since she couldn’t take it home. It was her favorite from their camping trip. He said it was his favorite photo of her and gave her a copy of it. I’m sure there were others of the two of them but she never showed them to me. That reminds me.” Hope got to her feet. “She left some stuff here. I thought you might—”

“I’d like it, please,” Mo said and they waited as the woman disappeared through a door and returned moments later with a large manila envelope.

“I don’t know what’s in it. I never looked.” She handed it to Mo. “Tricia said I should give it to you if anything happened to her.”

“Are you serious?” Mo demanded. “When were you going to tell me about this?” She clutched the envelope to her chest and glared at the woman.

“If you hadn’t been such a bitch at the funeral—”

“I’m curious. Why the secrecy?” Brick interrupted. “Why wouldn’t Tricia tell you the man’s name since she told you everything else?”

Hope shrugged again. "I wondered about that, too. I think he was somebody, you know? A name that either I would know or would have heard of. She was so worried that Thomas would find out and maybe do something to him."

"Or she thought you wouldn't have been able to keep her secret," Mo said, still clearly angry.

Hope glared back at her. "At least I knew what was going on." She raised a brow as if to say, *and she was your sister.*

Brick surreptitiously pocketed the photo he'd taken from the mantel and quickly got them both out of there.

Once in the pickup and driving again, Brick said, "This makes me wonder if Natalie wasn't telling the truth about all of it. You knew her. You liked her. She was worried about your sister, worried about Joey. She tried to warn you about what was going on. She was even convinced that Tricia didn't commit suicide and swears that she didn't harm Joey."

"What is the point of debating it now? She's dead." All she could think was that caught in this heartbreaking triangle and filled with guilt over Joey's paternity and health, her sister could have been in such an emotional state that she had killed herself.

"She wasn't lying about Tricia having an affair," he pointed out. "I don't think she was lying about your sister not killing herself."

"I don't know," Mo said, the manila envelope rest-ing unopened in her lap. She saw him check his rear-view mirror and not for the first time. "What is it?"

"We're being followed and have been since we left Hope's house."

Chapter Twelve

"You were right," the PI said into his hands-free device. "She went by the house. She was in there a good half hour. I'm following her and the deputy now."

He swore as he realized that he'd been spotted. "I'm going to have to let them get ahead of me." He turned at the next street. He was pretty sure where he could catch up to them again.

"How did they seem when they came out of the house?"

"Hard to say." He got paid to spy on people, photograph them, follow them. He didn't get paid to analyze their feelings, but he was smart enough not to say that. "Subdued." He could hear that the answer didn't make his client happy.

Ahead, he saw the pickup, but this time he stayed back. "They've pulled into a motel and are going inside the office." He told his employer the name of the downtown Billings motel as he pulled over to wait. "What would you like me to do? It appears they have booked a room and are now carrying their bags there."

"One room?"

"Yes, they both went into the same room." Jim listened for a moment. "Right, I can do that. I'll put the tracking device on the pickup tonight." Now that they knew they were being followed, he couldn't let them see him again.

"Once I can track them myself, I think it would be best if I took it from here."

"You're the boss."

"I'll stop by your office and pay you in cash when I pick up any file you might have made on this."

The man was worried that hiring a private detective to follow a homicide cop and a deputy marshal might come back on him?

"I understand." He hung up, telling himself he was glad to be done with this one. But just to cover his own behind, he'd keep a digital copy of his work and the man's requests. Hopefully, he would never have to use it, he thought as he waited for it to get dark enough to go back to the motel and attach the tracking device to Deputy Marshal Brick Savage's pickup.

"I'M NOT SURE I'm up to understanding any of this," Mo said once they were settled into the motel room and she'd taken a peek inside the envelope. She was exhausted—and still upset. Her sister had told Hope to give it to her in case anything happened to her. What had Hope been thinking? Clearly the woman didn't have a brain the size of a pea.

But what scared her was the realization that Tricia had known there was a chance that something *would* happen to her. So she'd left whatever was in this envelope for Mo. If only Hope had given it to her right away.

"What is it?" Brick asked as he pulled back the curtain to look out into the street.

"A stack of photocopied financial reports," she said. "I can't make heads or tails of them, not tonight." She wasn't sure what she'd hoped to find in the envelope. A diary. Photos. A suicide note. Something personal to Mo to explain what it was that she'd left for her. It made her question if Tricia had been in her right mind. Wasn't that her fear? That Natalie hadn't killed the baby? The only other person in the house that day was Tricia.

"I'm tired, too," Brick said as he checked outside again.

"Have you seen the vehicle that you thought was following us?" she asked, putting the manila envelope into her suitcase.

"No, maybe I was just being paranoid."

"Or letting Natalie get to you," Mo said with a sigh. "I'll wash up and go to bed."

Brick moved away from the window and stretched out on top of his bed.

By the time she came out of the bathroom, he was sound asleep. She crawled between the sheets in the matching queen bed. She couldn't quit thinking about her sister. Had Tricia fallen in love with the mystery man? That she would even have an affair was so unlike her, it was hard to believe. Tricia had always been the good one. It was one of the reasons she had gone to their grandmother's instead of Mo.

She closed her eyes, desperately wanting to put the day behind her. Natalie was dead. Whatever secrets the woman had refused to give up would go to the grave with her. She felt sleep tugging at her. Her last thought was that she hadn't gotten a chance to tell her sister goodbye.

Mo came out of the dream screaming. She felt hands on her and fought to shove them off, but the fingers were like steel.

"Mo. *Mo?*" The hands gave her a shake, and she opened her eyes, startled and instantly embarrassed because she knew she'd had another one of her dreams.

Brick released her and she sat up, backing against the headboard as she chased away the last of the darkness. They'd hardly spoken after renting the motel room. Mo didn't remember falling asleep but it must have been quickly.

She gulped air and tried to still her pounding heart. A chill in the room dried the perspiration on her skin, but her nightshirt still felt damp. As the light on in the room chased away the dark shadows that followed her sleep, she began to breathe easier.

"Better?" Brick asked now. He was sitting on the edge of the bed, but no longer touching her.

She nodded, unable to look at him. The nightmares were terrifying and embarrassing. They made her feel weak. Worse, vulnerable.

"A bad one, huh? I've had a few that followed

me into daylight," he said quietly. "The worst ones don't go away easily. They always make me afraid to close my eyes again because I know the terror is waiting for me."

She glanced in his direction and saw that he was looking at the hideous mountain painting on the opposite wall instead of at her. Her heart seemed to fill. He understood what she was going through because he'd not only had the bad dreams, but also he'd felt the weakness, the vulnerability, the embarrassment of them.

"If it helps, I can leave the light on," he said when he finally did look at her.

Mo shook her head. As he started to get up from her bed to turn off the lamp next to them, she touched his hand. She hadn't meant to reach for him. It was as if an inner need was stronger than she was. She hated needing anyone and yet she did.

"I can turn out the light and stay here, if you want me to," he said quietly.

She nodded, tears filling her eyes. She wiped at her the wetness on her face, heard him turn off the light, then felt his weight settle in next to her on the bed. She took a few calming breaths before she slid down in the bed to lie next to him.

Staring at the ceiling in the ambient light coming through the motel room's curtains, she felt him take her hand in his large warm one. Until that moment, she hadn't realized that she was trembling. But as he held her hand, she felt his warmth move through her until she quit shaking, until she was no longer afraid to close her eyes.

Brick woke with Mo snuggled against him and his arm around her. He didn't dare move, not wanting to wake. Not wanting to let her go just yet. He wondered about her bad dreams and was glad she hadn't had another one later last night.

With a shock he realized that he hadn't had one since the two of them had joined forces. Maybe he really was getting better. He smiled to himself and felt her shift in his arms. He held his breath.

"I know you're awake," she whispered.

"How can you tell?" he asked.

"Because your hand isn't on my breast anymore."

Brick withdrew his arms as she turned to face him. "I'm sorry, if I did anything—"

"I was joking," she said smiling. "You were a perfect gentleman." She eyed him as if surprised by that. And maybe…disappointed? "Should I be insulted?"

He chuckled. "Trust me, it's not because I haven't wanted to."

She laughed and turned to get up on the opposite side of the bed. "Trust you?" she said, her back to him. "Won't that be the day. I'm going to get a shower." She stopped and turned. "Have you ever carved your initials into a tree along with the name of one of your…women?"

"No."

Mo nodded and smiled. "I'm anxious to find that tree. I'm assuming you'll want to go along?" She said it over her shoulder as she headed for the bathroom.

"I'm stuck to you like glue," he said before she closed the door.

They spent the morning canvassing the neighborhood around Tricia and Thomas's house. Brick knew Mo was hoping that one of the neighbors might have seen a man going into the house who wasn't Thomas over the weeks that Tricia had been having the affair—or on the day she'd died.

When they came up empty, they stopped for lunch and then headed toward Red Lodge in hopes of finding the campsite where Tricia's lover had left their initials carved in a tree.

THEY ARRIVED AT the forest service campground midmorning. Most of the sites were open. A few occupants in tents and small trailers were packing up to leave as he drove slowly through the pines higher up the mountain.

He had the photograph that Tricia's alleged lover had taken on their camping trip.

On the way to the campground, Mo had been looking through the envelope her sister had left for her. Now she put it away, apparently still not understanding why Tricia wanted her to have it.

"I'm still shocked that we are looking for the identity of my sister's lover," Mo confided. "Tricia was always the rule follower, the voice of reason. For her to do this..."

"People fall in love," he said. "At least that's what I've heard."

She swung her gaze on him. "You've never been in love?"

He seemed as surprised by the question as she was

shocked that he hadn't been in love. He slowly drove through another loop of the campground. "Why? Have you?"

"Middle school, my science teacher. High school, this sweet boy who wrote me these awful poems. A couple of times in college. Several since then."

He laughed. "That's your love life?"

"Apparently, it's better than yours. You've really never been in love?"

He could feel her gaze on him as he pulled over and cut the engine in an empty campsite. "There's a tree down," he said in explanation for stopping. "We're going to have to walk to see the upper end of the campground, where we should have a view of the creek that's in the photo."

"You didn't answer my question," she said, keeping him from exiting the truck cab. "You weren't in love with even one of the women you dated?"

"I cared about all of them. Maybe you and I have a different definition of love. When I tell a woman that I love her it will be right before I propose marriage." With that, he climbed out of the pickup and closed the door.

Mo exited the truck as well, still looking surprised by his answer. They started up the mountain road, climbing over downed trees and limbs. "Looks like they had a storm up this way," he said. This high up the mountain, there were only the sounds of birds, the breeze high in the tops of the pines and the whisper of the stream. As they climbed higher, though, the sound of a roaring creek grew louder.

"Seriously, you've never felt…love?" she asked.

"The head over heels kind?" He shook his head and glanced at her. "I'm assuming you haven't, either. It's probably why you can't understand what happened to your sister."

She seemed to consider that. "You're probably right. It seems…reckless, something Tricia never was. At least I thought that was true. Let me see the photo." He handed it to her. "I think that's it up there," she said excitedly. "See that mountain in the distance?" She held up the snapshot.

"Lead the way," he agreed as they quickened their pace. Now all they had to do was find a tree up here with Tricia and her lover's initials carved in it.

As they reached the campsite, Mo stopped to check the photo again. "This is the campsite." She turned to see Brick already checking trees.

For a moment, she merely stood looking at this beautiful sight. The creek cut a green swath through the rocks and pines to fall away down the mountainside below them. She breathed in the rich, sweet scent of pine and caught a hint of someone's campfire smoke trailing up from a site below.

She thought of her sister, the last person she could imagine enjoying camping. That Tricia might have slept up here in the blue tent in the photo… It boggled the mind. She tried to imagine the man who could sweep her sister off her feet.

"Mo? I think you'd better come over here," Brick said.

She turned to find him standing next to a large pine tree at the edge of the mountainside, overlooking the roaring of the creek. As she approached, she saw the crude heart carved into the bark of the pine.

There were two sets of initials at the center of the heart. TM, a plus sign, and JP. Tricia's lover had used her maiden name initial. Wishful thinking on his part? Or was that the last name she'd given him? This man had understood from the beginning that Tricia was married, hadn't he?

"Know anyone with those initials?" Brick asked.

Mo shook her head. "I have no idea who JP is."

The gunshot echoed through the trees, splintering the bark on the tree next to her. Several nearby birds took flight, wings flapping wildly as Brick lunged for her, taking them both to the ground.

The second shot ricocheted off the tree where they had been standing, sending bark flying again. And then there was nothing but the sound of the breeze in the pines and seemingly hushed roar of the creek. Not even the birds sang for a moment as Mo tried to catch her breath.

Chapter Thirteen

In the distance, Brick heard an automobile engine start up. Through the trees he caught a flash of silver as the vehicle sped off, the sound dying as whoever had taken the potshots at them drove away.

Mo was on her feet as quickly as he was, the two of them running back down the road to where they'd left the truck. They had to slow down to climb over the downed trees and limbs, but finally reached the pickup.

Brick started it and drove as fast as he could out of the campground. By the time they reached the highway, there was no sign of the vehicle they'd glimpsed through the pines.

"Whoever that was, wasn't driving the black SUV that had been following us yesterday," Brick said. "What I want to know is how they knew we were going to the campsite?"

"Hope? You think she lied about knowing the man's name. She could have called him to tell him what she'd told us? That would be pretty stupid of her, wouldn't it? Especially if Tricia's lover is the one who just shot at us."

Brick pulled off his Stetson and raked a hand through his hair. "Then how did anyone know where to find us?"

"She must have told someone, unless…" Mo met Brick's gaze across the cab of the pickup. "You don't think…"

"I do think." He pulled the pickup to the side of the road and they both got out to search the undercarriage. They found the tracking device quickly enough. Brick was about to destroy it when Mo stopped him.

"Let's give whoever did this something to follow," she said, pointing to the freight train moving slowly along the tracks on the other side of the road.

Brick smiled and spotted a dirt road that ran beside the train track. Back in the truck, he drove along a narrow road along the tracks. Heading off the slow-moving freight train, he jumped out of the truck and waited for it to catch up to him. He was back to the pickup within minutes.

"All done." His gaze locked with hers. He was still shaken by the close call on the mountain. "Any idea what is going on?"

"I think we're getting close to the truth." She shook her head. "But I'm nowhere near figuring out who JP might be or what these documents are that Tricia left me."

"I need to go back up the mountain to get that

one slug that lodged in the tree," he said. "That is, if we're going to take this to the police."

Mo shook her head. "It's a long shot we could ever track it to the gun, but at least we will have the evidence."

He drove back up the mountain. "Why don't you wait here? I won't be long." He pulled his spare pistol out from under the seat of his truck and handed it to her. "Fire a shot if you need me."

She smiled. "You just handed me a loaded gun. I think I'll be able to take care of myself."

He wasn't gone long before he returned with the slug he'd dug out of the tree with his pocketknife.

"Do you think the person who shot at us was trying to kill us or just scare us?" she asked.

Brick smiled. "If he was trying to kill us, then he was a piss-poor shot. I think he was trying to send us a message."

"To quit looking for the man Tricia was involved with? Or stop looking for her killer?"

"Could be one and the same," Brick said.

Mo made a disgruntled sound. "All he did was make me more determined—and more convinced that what Natalie told me was true. Tricia didn't kill herself."

"He? The shooter could be a woman."

"My money is on her boyfriend. Who else would be worried about us finding out his identity?"

He could tell that Mo had been racking her brain, trying to figure out who JP could be while he was up on the mountain getting the slug.

"I can't even imagine how Tricia crossed paths with him between taking care of her house and her day job, though," she said.

"What is it?" Brick asked as he saw her freeze and then hurriedly pull out her phone.

"Something Hope said." She scrolled on her phone for a moment before she looked up. "My sister volunteered every other Saturday at a nonprofit dog shelter. I remember Thomas complaining that she spent more time there than at home and had to shower before he could get near her."

"Any luck?" he asked as he watched her thumb through the shelter site.

She shook her head. "No one on the board with those initials. I'm going to call Hope. Maybe the initials mean something to her." When Hope answered, she put the cell on speakerphone.

"We found the campsite and the carving on the tree of the heart with their initials in it. Do you remember anyone from college with the initials JP?"

"*JP?* No. Honestly, I've always thought it was Andy. He's such a sweetie and he's always liked her."

"Think. Do you know anyone by those initials?"

Hope was quiet for a moment. "Sorry, I don't. Tricia always referred to him as her special friend."

MO HUNG UP and put her phone away, irritated with Hope and even more irritated with herself. If she'd let Natalie tell her what was going on that day, she could have talked to Tricia. At least she would have tried to help her rather than hiding her head in the sand, not wanting to hear that anything was wrong.

"I'll call my partner at homicide when we get back to Billings," she said. "We can give him the slug you dug out of the tree—although I doubt it will lead us to the shooter. But I want to get everything I can on my sister's death."

An hour later, Mo introduced Brick to her partner, Lou Landry, outside the diner around the corner from Billings PD. A little gray around the edges and highly seasoned after thirty-five years at this, Lou was more like a father figure than a partner. Mo knew she'd been placed with him so he could keep her out of trouble. It had worked—until the Natalie Berkshire case.

"You are opening up a can of worms," Lou said after she told him what she needed. "Are you sure you want to do this?"

"I have to know if what Natalie Berkshire told me was true."

"Mo, I probably shouldn't be telling you this, but we are getting inquiries from all over the state and even the country about Natalie. It's much worse than we first thought. People are demanding the cases be reopened. They want answers and quite frankly it appears there is only one answer. Natalie Berkshire was a serial murderer."

"She swore she didn't kill Joey." She saw his pitying look.

"Just as she swore that your sister didn't kill herself?"

"At least I know that Natalie didn't have anything to do with Tricia's death. She was behind bars when Tricia hung herself."

Lou shook his head. "I'll get you the autopsy report, but I don't think you're going to find any answers in it. The coroner ruled it a suicide. If there had been anything suspicious—"

"I want to see the photos taken at the scene, as well."

He sighed. "Why put yourself through that?"

"Because I can't close that door until I'm sure."

"All right. I'll meet you back here in thirty minutes."

"Lou…thank you."

"What are partners for?" His expression saddened. "You're not coming back to the force, are you?"

"I don't know."

He nodded. "Thirty minutes." And he was gone.

She looked at Brick.

"He seems like a nice guy."

"He is."

"Are you really never going back?"

She shrugged. "Buy me a cup of coffee?" As they entered the diner, she saw Shane Danby and several of his friends leaving. Her stomach dropped, half expecting him to make a scene. To her surprise, he merely nodded and left.

Thirty minutes later, Lou entered the coffee shop and handed her a paper sack. "I hope you know what you're doing," he said and left.

Mo glanced into the sack and saw a copy of the

autopsy report and the photos taken at the scene. She closed the bag and turned to Brick. "I thought we could take these back to the motel. But first I need to use the ladies' room."

"I'll be waiting for you outside," he said, looking worried. Like Lou. Both knew that seeing the report and the photos was going to hit her hard. But she had to know. Since her sister's death and Joey's, she'd been having the nightmares. She had to believe that the reason for them was that justice hadn't been meted out. Not yet anyway.

BRICK STEPPED OUTSIDE the coffee shop into the summer sun. He was worried about Mo with good reason, he thought as he started down the street to where he'd parked his pickup. The threat against her was real. Someone had taken potshots at them. And now she was looking into her sister's death. Had they been followed to the campsite outside of Red Lodge?

He'd watched for a tail and hadn't spotted one. Who else knew about Tricia having been there? Who else knew about the carving on the tree with the initials on it? Tricia's lover.

"Well, look who it is?" said a male voice as he walked past an alley near where he'd left his truck. He'd been so lost in thought that he hadn't seen the man. Turning, he saw cop Shane Danby and two other men. Clearly, the three had been waiting for him. "Guess we meet again."

"What a coincidence," Brick said. "And you're

looking for trouble just like last time, only this time you brought your friends to help you."

Shane's jaw muscles bunched along with his fists as he took a step closer. "You should have stayed out of it with me and Mo. You messed with the wrong man." He took a swing, but Brick easily sidestepped it.

"Get him!" Shane cried and charged, head down. Brick caught him in an uppercut that knocked the man to his knees, but then Shane's buddies were on him. One slammed a fist into his lower back, knocking the wind out of him, as the other grabbed him in a headlock from behind.

He tried to fight them off as Shane got to his feet again and attacked with both fists before the cop's friends threw Brick to the ground. As he tried to get to his feet, Shane kicked him in the side, then the stomach, then in the head.

Brick heard the sound of sirens as he fought not to black out.

"He's a cop, man," one of his friends said as he pulled Shane away to keep him from kicking Brick again.

"I didn't know he was a cop," Shane said as he stumbled over to him and pulled his wallet out. "I was just walking by and the bastard attacked me. The two of you saw it. I didn't know he was some deputy marshal until I pulled his ID and by then, I had arrested him."

"That's your story?" one of Shane's friends demanded.

"That's *our* story," Shane snapped.

"You are going to get us into so much trouble," his friend complained.

"I already called in the attack," Shane said with a laugh. "A disturbance in an alley near Henry's Bar. Might need medical attention. Cops attacked."

As the cop car came roaring up, siren blaring and lights flashing, Shane said, "Just stick to the story." Walking past Brick, the cop got in one more kick.

Just before he passed out, Brick heard Mo's angry voice and then she was taking his truck keys as he was being carried to the cop car. The last thing he heard was her saying, "Don't worry, I'll get you out."

MO HAD WANTED TO attack Shane herself. Instead, she demanded that Brick be given medical attention, promising to bail him out as quickly as she could.

"Shane, you best watch your back," she warned him quietly as Brick was loaded into the back of the ambulance behind the police cruiser.

"You aren't threatening an officer of the law, are you, Mo?" He smirked at her. "Careful, or you'll end up behind bars, as well."

She'd already been behind bars, so she kept her mouth shut. This was all her fault. If she hadn't involved Brick in this… If he hadn't come to her rescue at the bar… Through her anger, she told herself that there was nothing else she could do for Brick. He wouldn't be arraigned until tomorrow at the earliest. All she could do was wait and then get him out on bail—just as he'd done for her.

In the meantime, she had the autopsy report and

the photos, and she knew the initials of Tricia's lover. It wasn't much, but there had be something in them to prove that Tricia hadn't taken her own life. Once she did that, she wouldn't let it go until her sister's murderer was caught.

Storming over to Brick's pickup, she climbed in and tossed the paper sack Lou had given her onto the seat. It toppled over, spilling some of the contents onto the floor.

Mo saw one photo of her sister, the noose around her neck, and burst into tears. She leaned over the steering wheel, letting it all out. For weeks, she'd used her anger keep her from releasing the pain inside her. Now it overflowed with chest-aching sobs, the dam breaking.

After a few minutes, she gulped and wiped furiously at her face. Finally under control, she leaned down to pick up everything that had fallen. She was shoving it all back into the paper sack when she realized the paper in her hand hadn't come out of the bag Lou had given her.

She stared down at the sheet of paper. It took her a moment to realize what she was looking at—the flyer Thomas's associate Quinn had handed her outside the jail. Something caught her eye. She smoothed out the sheet of paper.

Jeffrey Palmer, the self-made man and seminar speaker. JP. She remembered Thomas talking about the wonderful speakers his company always managed to book. Hadn't Tricia gone to one of these with her husband?

The multimillionaire's list of accomplishments was a mile long. She stared at his photograph. He had to be pushing seventy with thick gray hair and bushy gray eyebrows. This man couldn't have been Tricia's lover, could he?

Jeffrey Palmer was hosting a cocktail party the last night of the conference at his home in Big Sky. She was telling herself that it was just a coincidence that the man had the same initials as Tricia's lover when she turned the flyer over and froze.

In this photograph, Jeffrey Palmer Sr. stood next to his son, Jeffrey "JP" Palmer Jr. Her gaze dropped to the cutline under the photograph. Palmer and his son had received the governor's award for a nonprofit corporation they'd started called My Son's Dream, an animal sanctuary.

Her heart began to pound harder. My Son's Dream. MSD, Inc. The animal shelter where Tricia had volunteered. Mo remembered a baseball cap with MSD, Inc., on it that her sister had worn to a picnic last summer.

She looked closer at the photo of JP. According to his bio, he was just a year older than Mo. The closer she looked at him, she realized she recognized him. He'd changed considerably since college. He'd filled out, no longer wore thick dark-rimmed glasses, and his dull brown hair was now blond. In college, he'd gone by Junior.

Like Hope, Jeffrey junior had always been at the periphery of the group that she and Tricia had hung out with. So Hope would have known Jeffrey junior, but probably wouldn't have remembered him by JP any more than Mo had.

Was it possible this was Tricia's lover? It had to be. It was his animal shelter that Tricia had worked at. She recalled Thomas complaining about how much time she spent down there. That had to be where they'd met, and hadn't Hope said that Tricia and her lover had shared a soft spot for animals?

Her heart was a drum in her chest. She recalled Hope saying that Tricia and her lover had joked about how much Thomas loved Jeffrey Palmer's seminars. The pieces of the puzzle fit.

"I've got you, JP," she said as she started the pickup. Now all she had to do was find out why her sister had wanted her to have the papers she'd left for her. They must have meant something to Tricia. Mo had a friend, Elroy, in finance.

Thirty minutes later, she dropped off the papers. Elroy promised to get back to her. She thought about waiting until she got Brick out on bail before she confronted JP, but that would be so not like her, she thought as she drove out to the animal shelter.

Chapter Fourteen

Brick sat on the cot in the cell, worrying about Mo. He knew she could take care of herself. But he also knew how emotionally involved she was in finding out the truth about her sister's death. That alone could put her off her usual guard. Not to mention, they'd already been shot at. He no longer doubted that they had been on the trail of a killer. A killer who now knew that Mo was after him.

At the rattle of his cell door, he looked up to find a guard standing there. "Phone call," the man said, not sounding happy about it as he unlocked the door. "Come on."

In a small office off the cell block, he took the phone that was handed to him. "Hello?" He was hoping to hear Mo's voice. But his gut told him there could be only one person calling. He closed his eyes at the sound of his father's voice.

"What the hell, Brick?"

He turned his back to the guard, keeping his voice down. "I was jumped in the alley by three cops. Believe me, I didn't start this."

Marshal Hud Savage sighed. "Maybe it's the best place for you right now."

"It's not." He glanced at the cop standing by the door. "Mo is out there trying to find her sister's murderer. I'm worried about her."

"I'm worried about *you.*"

"Mo will get me out once I see a judge."

"Brick, if you're serious about keeping your job—"

"I'll take care of this." There were witnesses at the bar when Shane attacked Mo and he had hopes that the other two cops would tell the truth when push came to shove. But this wouldn't look good on his record if he couldn't convince a judge of his innocence.

MO REALIZED THAT she would have never connected JP with the young man she remembered from college. Seeing this version of the man, she could understand how Tricia might have fallen for him. He had broad, well-developed shoulders and had apparently traded the glasses for contacts, and his face was ruggedly handsome, all sign of his bouts of acne long gone under his tan.

But the shyness was still there. Mo could see where Tricia would have found it charming. She watched him move through the crowd, greeting people as he went. Apparently the shelter was having a fund-raiser this evening. Mo thought of all the organizations father and son were involved in, including MSD, Inc. But it was the shelter that would have helped steal Tricia's heart.

When he reached her, she saw the sparkle of surprise in his blue eyes. She hadn't expected him to remember her. But then again, if he'd been having an affair with her sister…

"Maureen," he said and reached for her hand, cupping it in both of his large ones. "It is so good to see you. I didn't realize you were an animal lover."

"Not as much as my sister, Tricia, I'm sure."

His eyes narrowed slightly, but his smile remained in place. "Let's step into my office." She followed him down a thick-carpeted hallway lined with framed professional photographs of adorable animals.

Everything about this part of the shelter felt lavishly done so she wasn't surprised when he opened the door to his office. It had the same polished, rich look to it from the shine of the huge mahogany desk to the well-appointed other furnishings.

"We're having a little thank-you party for some of our donors, so I don't have much time to spare." He closed the door behind him. "Please have a seat," he said as he motioned to one of the chairs in front of the desk. He took his seat behind the desk. "Can I get you some coffee, water, champagne?"

"I'm good, thanks," she said as she sank into the soft leather. "It's been a long time." She considered him. "You've changed."

He chuckled. "Just on the outside. I'm still that shy, tongue-tied awkward guy I was in college."

She highly doubted that and said as much.

Leaning back, he seemed to study her. "I didn't think you ever knew who I was at college."

She knew that Tricia would have been impressed by these surroundings. JP, like his father, had made something out of himself and he was saving animals. It would have been a deadly combination.

"But my sister would have remembered you," she said. "When the two of you ran into each other here at the shelter."

His eyes lost some of the blue twinkle. "She told you about us?"

"No, *you* did. The heart you carved in the tree at the campground above Red Lodge. You used her maiden name initial. TM plus JP. Instead of *C* for her married name, Colton. You did know she was married, right?" She saw the answer in his expression. "Mortensen was the name you'd known her by in college, but I guess I don't have to tell you that."

"She didn't pay any more attention to me in college than you did, but we realized we knew some of the same people."

Was that bitterness she heard in his voice? "Is that why you decided to ruin her marriage and ultimately her life?"

He sat forward so abruptly it startled her. "I *loved* her. I still love her." His voice broke and tears flooded his eyes. "It just happened. Working here together, we fell in love. We didn't mean for it to happen."

She looked around his posh office for a moment. "Did your father know about you and Tricia?"

He sat back again. "Why would you ask that?"

She said nothing and waited, her gaze coming back to him.

Finally, he said, "My father wasn't happy about my falling in love with a married woman, no. But I didn't care and I told him as much. I was going to marry her and we were going to raise our son together."

"*Your* son?" She stared at him. "Joey was your son?"

"I don't know that he was mine biologically. It didn't matter. As far as I was concerned, he was ours no matter what."

"That's very noble," she said, unable to keep the sarcasm out of her voice.

"I told you. I loved her. I would have done anything for her. *Anything*."

"Where did the two of you get together besides here?" she asked, having seen the inviting leather couch off to one side of the room.

He sighed. "Does it really matter?"

She narrowed her gaze on him. "It does to me."

"My father has a cabin outside of Red Lodge." She could just imagine what Jeffrey Palmer Sr.'s *cabin* was like. "Are these questions really necessary? Your sister is—"

"Dead. Yes, I know. When did Tricia break it off?" She waited and when he didn't answer, she said, "She did break it off, right? You must have been upset."

"Of course I was upset. She told me she was pregnant with Thomas's son. I knew she couldn't know that for sure. But it was clear she wanted Joey to be his. She was determined to make her marriage work as if she had to pay penitence for falling in love with me."

"But even after she broke it off, the two of you were still seeing each other," Mo said.

He looked away for a moment. "We couldn't stay away from each other. I wanted her to tell Thomas. I was sick of lying and hiding in the shadows. I wanted everyone to know how much I loved her."

"You must have been angry when she wouldn't."

JP groaned. "What are you getting at? You think me putting pressure on her drove her to suicide?"

"Do you think she killed herself?"

He went stone cold still, his eyes widening. "I… I was told that she did. Are you telling me she didn't?"

She didn't take her gaze from his face. "I think there's a chance someone murdered her."

JP looked as if he was in shock. He stood up, but then sat back down. His gaze ricocheted around the room before falling on her again. "She was *murdered*?" He seemed genuinely shocked.

"I don't have any proof. Yet."

He stared at her. "Then why would you say something like that?"

"Natalie. She told me it wasn't suicide."

"How would Natalie know?" When she said nothing, he continued as if trying to work it out himself. "Tricia didn't accidentally hang herself. Though Natalie certainly isn't the most reliable source." Mo realized that JP hadn't heard about Natalie's death. He'd just referred to her in the present. "But if Natalie is telling the truth..." His gaze locked with hers. "I always feared what Thomas would do when he found out."

"But he wasn't going to find out—not unless you told him," Mo said. She thought of what Natalie had written in the note. "After Joey was born, she refused to see you again, didn't she? Natalie witnessed your argument."

Mo watched his expression sour. She could see the answer in the hard glint of his blue eyes. He tapped his freshly manicured nails on the edge of the desk for a moment before balling his hands into fists. She could see him fighting to get control again.

"Tricia was a mess. She blamed herself for Joey's medical problems. She thought it was karma, payback. I tried to reason with her... We were so right for each other. We loved each other. We belonged together." He looked down, saw his tightly fisted hands and quickly relaxed them.

Mo thought of how stubborn her sister could be. "I take it she wouldn't listen to reason?"

He scoffed. "She didn't want to break Thomas's heart. My heart was another story." His hands had fisted again and his blue eyes had gone dark. He met her gaze, and in that moment she saw a man capable of murder.

Chapter Fifteen

Back in downtown Billings, Mo went to work to free Brick. She canvassed the neighborhood near the coffee shop until she found what she was looking for—a surveillance camera that had caught everything that happened in the alley.

"I'd prefer to handle this in-house," the chief of police told her after he'd watched the surveillance video she'd copied to her phone. He'd watched it twice before swearing and handing her phone back. She knew this wasn't the first time there had been complaints against Shane Danby. "Email me that," he said gruffly. "We should talk about you coming back to work."

Mo got to her feet. "I appreciate everything you've done for me—"

"I'm not accepting your resignation if that's what you're about to say. Mo, I know how hard all this has been on you. You need time, so take as much as you want. Please, don't make a hasty decision."

She nodded. "Thank you. Can you release Deputy Marshal Brick Savage for me?"

He groaned. “What the hell was Shane thinking? A deputy marshal whose father is the marshal at Big Sky?” Shaking his head, he picked up the phone and called down. Hanging up, he turned to her again. “He’s all yours.”

She smiled at that.

“By the way, I’m not sure what the two of you are up to…” He waited as if he’d hoped she would fill in the blanks.

“We’re just friends enjoying a Montana summer together.”

Her boss groused. “Have it your way.”

Downstairs, Mo was waiting as Brick was brought out. She grimaced at his swollen black eye, the bandaged cut on his temple, a split lip and the bruise on his cheek. She could tell from the way he was moving that his ribs were bruised. She hoped she didn’t run into Shane in a dark alley because she knew it would take a half-dozen men to pull her off him.

Not wanting Brick to see how shocked she was by his injuries or how furious it made her, she joked, “We really have to quit meeting like this.”

He smiled even with his cut lip. “Good to see you, too.”

“This is all my fault,” she said. “If I hadn’t got into it with Shane—”

“Nothing about this is your fault. He’s a bad cop. You already knew he was dangerous and he’s worse when he has two friends with him.”

“Well, all charges against you have been dropped. A surveillance camera on one of the businesses across from the alley caught it all. Shane will be lucky to keep his job, and the other two…" She shook her head. "Fools that they are, hopefully they'll wise up and put some distance between themselves and Shane. But I have good news."

"Sounds like you already gave me the good news," he said as she handed him his keys.

"I found JP," she said.

"YOU FOUND HIM?" Brick grinned at her as they walked out of the police station. She just kept amazing him. He couldn't believe how glad he was to see her—and not just because she'd gotten him out of jail. The moment he'd spotted her coming toward him, he'd felt his pulse kick up. When she smiled at him… What was it about this woman? She was often prickly as a cactus, annoyingly stubborn and impossible to reason with much of the time. But just the thought of this being over and never seeing her again…

He tried to concentrate on what she was telling him.

As she finished filling him in on her meeting with JP at the animal shelter, he felt sick. While he was behind bars, she'd risked her life. "You shouldn't have gone there alone. If there is even a chance that he's responsible for your sister's death—"

She laughed at that as they exited the building. "You keep forgetting that I'm a cop. I can take care of myself. Protecting me, well, that's not why I need you."

He felt heat rush to his veins and smiled as he

stopped to face her. "You need me?" He locked eyes with her for a few breathless moments.

She laughed. "You're growing on me, okay?"

He'd been fighting the urge to take her in his arms and kiss her for too long. He pulled her to him, his mouth dropping to hers. She melted into him as if she'd been made to fit there. Her lips parted as he pulled her closer, deepening the kiss and completely forgetting where they were until he heard cheering and clapping.

They pulled apart as a group of cops came out of the police station and headed for his pickup.

He opened her passenger-side door for her before he walked stiffly around to climb behind the wheel. When he looked over at Mo, he saw that her cheeks were flushed. "About the kiss—"

She cut him off. "I liked it, okay? Let's leave it at that for now."

He couldn't help his grin as he punched the key into the ignition. "So," he said, clearing his throat. "Do you think JP might be responsible for your sister's death?" Brick heard her settle into her side of the pickup cab. He wondered if her heart was pounding as hard as his was.

"I don't know. I think JP's life of privilege and his unrequited love for my sister makes him capable of murder. I want to talk to his father. The elder Jeffrey Palmer was not happy about the situation. I'm wondering what he might have done about it."

Her cell phone rang. She checked to see who it was and quickly picked up. "Elroy, tell me you made sense of those papers I gave you." She listened, nodding, then smiling over at Brick. "If you're sure that's what needs to be done. Just keep a copy of them for… insurance." She chuckled. "No, I don't trust anyone. And thanks again." As she disconnected, she looked like the cat who'd eaten the canary. "We definitely should talk to Jeffrey Palmer Sr."

"You aren't going to tell me?"

She merely smiled. "Let's see what Jeffrey says first."

He liked that there was no question about them not working together anymore. They were in it to the end. He just didn't like thinking about it ending.

"Jeffrey Palmer Sr. has a lodge near Lone Peak Mountain outside of Big Sky. I thought we could pay him a surprise visit."

Brick smiled over at her as he started the pickup. "Lucky me, I know the way."

"THE TRACKING DEVICE isn't working."

The PI sat up in bed, blinking as he tried to wake up. He'd been on an all-night surveillance trying to get the goods on a cheating husband and had just gotten to sleep when his cell phone had rung.

He started to ask, "Who is this?" but then he knew. He'd thought it was the last he'd be hearing from this client. "I put it on the deputy's truck."

"Well, you must have not gotten it right because I show the truck is on its way to the Midwest."

Jim groaned. "He must have discovered it." That could mean only one thing. "He must have caught you following him." Silence. He closed his eyes, cursing silently. This is why he hated to have clients take over the surveillance. They thought they could do this, but often learned the hard way that it wasn't that easy. Now his client had blown it.

"What can we do now?"

He opened his eyes, having been here before. "I might be able to find them but it will take time and money."

"Find them. I don't care what it costs."

The PI smiled. This was why he always put a second tracking device on the vehicle that only he could access on his phone. He knew it wouldn't be found because the first device was where it couldn't be missed. Once they found the first one, they never looked for a second.

"I'll do what I can." He hung up and reached for his phone to check the device. It appeared the deputy was headed home to Big Sky. Turning off the phone, Jim lay back down and closed his eyes. He would let the client stew for at least a few hours before he called to inform him of the cost before he told him where he could find the deputy.

A THUNDERSTORM MOVED across the tops of the mountains, smothering the sunlight and throwing the canyon in deep shadow as they neared Big Sky.

"I don't know about you, but I'm hungry," Brick said. He'd had breakfast in jail, but hadn't eaten since.

"I'm starved," Mo said and glanced around, surprised they were almost back to Big Sky. She realized she must have fallen asleep—and not had a nightmare. That alone surprised her almost as much as the earlier kiss. Oh, she'd known that Brick was going to kiss her. She'd been expecting it for some time.

What had come as a shock were the emotions the kiss had evoked. Not just desire. The deputy was drop-dead sexy. But the close feeling she'd felt. The safe, protected…loving feeling that had filled her. Was that why she hadn't had the nightmare?

That she'd even come close to thinking the *L* word scared her. She knew his reputation and she wasn't about to fall for him. Maybe she hadn't had the nightmare because she knew she was close to getting justice for her sister—if not for Joey.

"I know a great place to eat," Brick said and pulled out his phone. "I'll get us a reservation."

"Reservation?" She looked down at what she was wearing. "I'm not dressed for somewhere fancy."

"Trust me, you're dressed perfectly for this place." He grinned at her and even the approaching thunderstorm couldn't dampen the moment.

She smiled back at him, enjoying his enthusiasm. How easy it would be to fall for this man. She shook her head at that stray thought and realized the time. It was almost five in the afternoon. Whatever restaurant he called must have just opened for the evening.

"Great, we'll be there in about twenty minutes," he said into the phone and disconnected. "The special tonight is roast beef with mashed potatoes, freshly picked carrots in a butter sauce and chocolate cake for dessert."

She groaned. "You are making my mouth water."

"And what a mouth it is."

She felt heat rush to her cheeks and looked away, telling herself not to get caught up in his flirting. At the same time, she was glad to have Brick distracting her. For so long her mind had been dominated by getting justice. She was looking forward to a meal with this man. She'd actually missed him while he was locked up in jail—not that she'd admit it to him, she thought with a smile.

As he passed the exit to Big Sky, she wondered where this restaurant was that he was taking her to. A few miles later, he turned off the highway. The pickup bounced along the dirt road, over a bridge spanning the Gallatin River, and came to a stop in front of a large two-story ranch house. She saw barns and outbuildings, corrals and horses. Up on the mountain was a series of small cabins.

"Brick?" she asked as she took in the house again. This didn't look like a restaurant. As the front door opened and an older woman stepped out wearing an apron, Mo saw the resemblance immediately. "Is that your mother?"

"Best cook in four counties," he said, smiling as he got out of the pickup and came around to her side to open the door for her as if this was a date. She realized that to Brick, it was. Worse, he'd taken her home to meet his mother? And if that patrol car parked on the other side of the ranch pickup was any indication, it wasn't just his mother.

Mo cursed him under her breath. She was having dinner with the marshal and his wife? What had Brick been thinking?

Chapter Sixteen

"Mom, this is Mo," Brick said and quickly added, "Maureen Mortensen."

Dana smiled and reached for Mo's hand. "When my son called and asked about bringing a guest for dinner, I was delighted. I don't see enough of him and it is always wonderful to meet a friend of his."

Mo started to correct her about their relationship, but Brick cut her off as he put his arm around her and said, "I was just telling Mo that my mother is the best cook in four counties."

"Oh, you quit that," Dana said, letting go of Mo's hand to swat playfully at him. She frowned as she took in his injuries, but didn't say anything. No doubt she'd already heard he'd been in jail. "In case you haven't noticed, my son tends to exaggerate."

"I've noticed," Mo said and turned to gaze up at him, her blue eyes hot as a laser. "He's just full of surprises."

His mother cocked her head at him as if wondering about his relationship with this woman, but she was smiling as she ushered them both inside. "Your father should be here shortly. He's checking the new foal. I thought it would be nice to just have dinner with the four of us."

"Where's Angus and Jinx?" he asked as they entered the farmhouse with its wood floors, Native American rugs and antlers on the walls. The place never changed and that was what he loved about it. Coming here always felt like home. The house was cool even on the hot summer evening and rich with the scent of roast beef cooking in the kitchen.

"Your brother has Jinx up on the mountain, helping him at the house," Dana said and turned to Mo. "Angus and his wife are building a home on the ranch. I assume you haven't met either of them yet?" She looked to her son.

He shook his head. "We've been busy."

"So I've heard."

"Angus is my twin brother. I'm the charming one," Brick said. "I'm also the handsome one."

"Don't believe anything Brick says," his mother chided. "He just can't help himself." At the sound of the front door opening, she insisted they have a seat in the dining room while she saw to his father.

Brick knew what that meant. The marshal was unaware of their dinner guests.

"This was a very bad idea," Mo said under her breath as he steered her toward the huge table that took up most of the equally huge dining room.

"It's fine, trust me."

"There you go again thinking I'm going to trust you." She stopped short of the table and turned to face him. "And why are you letting your mother think that we're..."

"Lovers?"

Her eyes flared even hotter. "Involved."

"We *are* involved. And last night we slept together." He grinned to show that he was joking. "What does it matter what she thinks about our relationship?"

"It's not honest. And I like her. I don't want to lie to her."

He cocked an eyebrow at her. "I had no idea you were so straight-laced," he said, leaning close to whisper the words. "I'm beginning to wonder just about your relationships with those men you said you thought you had fallen in love with before."

"If you're asking what I think you are..." She gave him a shove. Brick chuckled, seeing her face redden charmingly before he realized they were no longer alone.

"Marshal," Mo said.

Brick turned to face his frowning father. "I guess Mom warned you that you have dinner guests."

"Everyone, please sit," his mother said, rushing into the room. "Brick's been bragging up my cooking, so I'd better get that roast out before it's overdone."

"Let me help you," Mo said and left Brick alone with his father, which he realized was her plan.

"I hate to even ask," Hud said.

"Then don't. I promised Mo a good meal with lively conversation."

His father harrumphed at that. "Not from me."

"Never from you," Brick said and laughed.

As the marshal moved toward his seat at the head of the table, he placed a hand on his son's shoulder and gave it a squeeze. "Glad to see you're still alive and not in jail."

"Me, too," he admitted as he hurried to help his mother with the huge platter of roast beef. She always cooked as if for an army so he'd known there would be plenty. Mo brought out bowls of towering fluffy mashed potatoes and freshly snapped and cooked green beans from his mother's garden as well as the buttered carrots.

As Brick pulled out a chair for Mo to sit, his mother ran back into the kitchen for the homemade rolls still warm from the oven, along with butter and honey.

"Brick, if you would pour the iced tea," she said as she took her seat on her husband's right. She always sat close to the kitchen in case anyone needed anything. He knew that one of the reasons she stayed in such good shape was that she kept so busy taking care of all of them.

And yet as the food was passed around and his mother kept the conversation going, he was reminded that both of his parents were at the age where they had started to slow down. He was glad that he'd come home to stay and could help out more.

"Interesting how you two met," his mother was saying.

"I sprung her from jail," Brick said. "Will make a fun story to tell our children."

Mo KICKED HIM under the table and said, "He is such a kidder, isn't he?"

"Isn't he though?" the marshal agreed, joining the conversation for the first time. "Are you about done with your…investigation?"

"We're getting it narrowed down," Brick said. "Tonight we're going to a cocktail party up on the mountain. Jeffrey Palmer Sr. is putting it on. Are you familiar with him?" he asked his father.

"Only by reputation."

Mo noticed that this part of the conversation had definitely piqued the marshal's interest, though.

"He's a very powerful man," the marshal said. "I hope—"

"That we'll be well behaved?" Brick said and laughed. "Always."

"Brick," Dana began, but was cut off.

"I've had the charges against Mo dropped," Hud to his son. "I believe the charges against you in Billings have also been dropped? I was hoping that would be the last of your combined jail times."

"Our hope, as well," Brick agreed.

Mo saw that the marshal's gaze was on her. "You still believe that your sister was murdered?"

She nodded, sorry that the conversation had taken this turn. She was enjoying the wonderful meal and pleasant conversation with Dana. She had liked her at once. What a warm, loving woman. No wonder Brick was the man he was.

"And where does Jeffrey Palmer fit into this?" the marshal asked.

"His son, JP, was having an affair with my sister," Mo said.

Hud sighed. "He's a suspect, but his father…?"

"His father knew about the relationship and disapproved," Mo said. "If he wanted my sister out of his son's life badly enough…" She didn't add what Elroy suspected about the financial papers Tricia had left for her. He was having a friend look at them and would get back to her.

The marshal leaned back in his chair, pushing his nearly empty plate away. "You two are scaring me. If you really believe either of these men is capable of murder…"

"We'll be careful," Brick said.

His mother rose to take their plates, announcing that there was chocolate cake for desert. Mo could see how nervous she was with this kind of talk. After all the years her husband had been in law enforcement, Mo would have thought that she'd gotten use to it. She got up to help with the cake.

"It's a cocktail party," Mo said, trying to relieve her concerns as she came into the kitchen. "There will be lots of people there. I'm sure there won't be any trouble."

Dana turned to look at her. "You know that I'm not delighted with Brick joining the marshal's department."

Mo nodded, seeing that she also wouldn't be delighted with having another cop in the family. "Brick and I aren't…in a romantic relationship."

The ranch woman smiled at her, the skin around

her eyes crinkling with humor. "I was going to say that I've accepted that Brick wants to follow the path his father took. I'll never get used to the discussions we've had around my dining room table, but I've also never seen Brick happier. Thank you." Dana reached for her hand and squeezed it. "We'd better get this cake out there and save my son from his father's interrogation."

Mo wanted to tell her that she wasn't responsible for Brick's happiness, but before she could, the woman pushed four dessert plates into her hands. Dana picked up the most beautiful chocolate layer cake Mo thought she'd ever seen before leading the way back into the dining room.

It wasn't until after dessert that Mo found herself alone with the marshal. She felt she had to say something into the heavy silence that had fallen over the room in Brick's and his mother's absence.

"I'm sure you're angry at me for getting your son involved in this," she said and waited.

Hud studied her openly for a moment, then shook his head. "Brick is his own man. He's always been determined to finish what he started. What worries me is that he's never brought a woman home. That he brought you home for one of his mother's meals… He's falling for you." He must have seen her surprise. "He jokes around, yes, but I know my son. All I ask is that you not break his heart since this is a first for him."

Their conversation ended abruptly as Brick and his mother returned from helping his mother with the dishes, something he'd insisted on. Clearly the two had been in silent alliance.

Mo had trouble following the rest of the conversation before she and Brick left for the cocktail party at Jeffrey Palmer Sr.'s. She kept thinking about what the marshal had said and wanting to deny—even to herself—how close she and Brick had gotten.

THE PI MADE the call earlier than he'd planned when another case took precedence. After the client wired him the extra fee, he said, "She returned to Big Sky." He held the phone away from his ear as his client let out a thunderbolt of curses.

"Why would she do that?"

Jim had to assume it was a rhetorical question since he didn't know the woman.

"Is she still with that deputy?"

"I can only suppose so. I just know that they returned to Big Sky. If you want more information—"

"I'll get it myself," the client snapped and disconnected.

The PI also disconnected and checked to see where the pickup was now. It appeared to be on the opposite side of the river from the town of Big Sky. He looked closer. It appeared to be at a ranch of some sort.

As he put away his cell phone, he realized that he knew where the deputy's pickup was, but he couldn't be sure that the female was still with him.

He shook his head as if to clear his thoughts. The client was determined to take it from here. He considered what he'd been hired to do over the past few days and tried to make sense of it before he stopped himself.

He often didn't understand why people did what they did. In all the years he'd been a private investigator, he'd found they often did the one thing they shouldn't because it was going to get them into trouble. But they still did it.

He had a feeling his client was about to do something that he would regret.

Jim was just glad he'd gotten his final payment before the fool either ended up dead or in jail. But he had to wonder why the man was so obsessed with the woman cop.

Chapter Seventeen

Jeffrey Sr. ushered them into his den, closing the door behind him before striding around to sit behind his desk. "I was surprised to hear that the two cops who crashed my cocktail party now want to speak to me in my office. Deputy Marshal Brick Savage and Homicide Detective Mo Mortensen?" He pretended to tip his hat to them each. "To what do I owe this honor since one of you is suspended and the other is on inactive duty, as I understand it?" Mo thought it interesting that the man had taken the time to check on both of them first. "So can I assume this isn't a professional visit?"

"Assume whatever you like," she said as she took a seat even though he hadn't offered her one. Brick remained standing next to her chair. "Your son was having an affair with my married sister."

The senior Jeffrey showed no reaction to her statement. She reached out and stroked the wings on the large sculpture of an eagle that graced his desk.

"I'm sure you were aware they were using your residence outside of Red Lodge for their...clandestine rendezvous." To her surprise, she saw that he hadn't been aware of that. His face clouded, eyes darkening, but he quickly recovered.

"If you're asking if I sanctioned such a…relationship, I did not."

"I believe it was at your Red Lodge home that Tricia learned something she shouldn't have. Something about one of your nonprofits that you didn't want the public to know." Still no response. "Knowing Tricia, she would have taken her concerns directly to you. I would imagine you alleviated her fears, but you couldn't trust that she might say something, so you went to her house that day. You knew Thomas wasn't there because he was at work. You're a big strong man. It wouldn't have taken much to see that she never talked. Although Tricia would have fought you. I suspect you drugged her, but that will come out once toxicology tests are run."

"Wasn't her body cremated?"

That this man knew that chilled her to the bone. "I guess you haven't heard. A scientist found a way to get evidence from a cremated body. I've turned Tricia's remains over to Forensics."

Did Jeffrey look paler? He wiped a spot on his upper lip that had turned shiny.

"The police had no reason not to believe it was a suicide after Tricia lost her baby—and maybe a hint that her marriage was on the rocks," Mo said. "How am I doing so far?"

"It's your tale," the man said, looking bored.

"Basically, you killed two birds with one stone. You weren't happy about your son and Tricia's relationship, especially with a baby involved. So that took care of that as well as making sure your secret never came out."

Jeffrey chuckled. "I'm much smarter than I thought since apparently I also got away with it because all of this is simply conjecture. If you had any proof, the *real* police would be here, right?"

"I can't prove that you killed her, but you definitely had motive."

Jeffrey sighed. "I really have no idea what you're talking about. What is it you want from me? I'm a busy man and my guests are waiting."

Mo pushed to her feet. "Nothing. I believe I'll have what I've come for soon. Justice for my sister."

She started to turn to leave but stopped. "By the way, those incriminating papers Tricia found in your study at the Red Lodge cabin? She made copies. She loved dogs and when she realized what you were using the nonprofit facility to do, she planned to stop you. But she must have told you that." She hesitated for a couple of beats. "Or maybe she only told your son. That kind of information could destroy you and JP if he knew about it. But I'm sure he denied everything to her—unless she didn't believe him. Oh, and the evidence? I put it somewhere safe with instructions that if anything should happen to me or anyone around me, it would be released to the FBI and the media—and not just locally."

With that she headed for the door. Behind her, she heard Jeffrey pick up the eagle sculpture from his desk. It shattered just feet from them as she and Brick walked out.

ONCE OUT IN the hallway, Brick swore as he spotted his father moving through the crowd. "My father is here. I need to see why—other than worrying about us."

"I could use some fresh air," Mo said. "I'm going to step out on the patio. Holler if you need me."

He chuckled at that. He would always need her, he thought, and quickly stepped away before he was fool enough to say it.

"Tell me you didn't follow us," Brick said as he stepped up behind his father.

The marshal turned, pretending surprise to see his son there. "I just came for the champagne."

Brick laughed. "Sure you did. Seriously," he said, lowering his voice. "What are you doing here?"

"It has nothing to do with you."

"Right."

"But I do wish that you and Mo would get out of here soon," his father said, glancing around.

Brick felt the hair prickle on the back of his neck. "You're here for a bust? *And arrest?* Is it—"

The marshal shot him a look that made him swallow back the words. He thought about what Mo had said to Jeffrey Sr. Did she really have some kind of evidence on him that would be worth killing to keep secret? Or had she been bluffing? The woman could craft a lie faster than anyone he'd ever met and yet…

He met his father's gaze. "I'll find Mo and we'll go."

AFTER BRICK LEFT to talk to his father, Mo had started for the doors out to the patio when she'd heard a voice directly behind her. She'd instantly tensed as she'd recognized it.

"We should step out on the patio." JP had placed his hand in the center of her back, his touch gentle but insistent.

Mo didn't put up a fight as he'd pushed open the patio doors and they exited the cocktail party. The patio was large, hanging over the side of the mountain, and the view was spectacular. The patio was also empty since the breeze was a reminder that the mountains around them were still snowcapped. Or maybe she felt the chill because she suddenly found herself alone on the edge of a precipice with a man who very possibly was a killer.

Jeffrey steered her to the edge, as far from the party as possible. "What are you doing here?" he demanded. He was dressed in formal attire and couldn't have been more handsome and distinguished. Her heart ached at the thought that if Tricia had seen him like this, she would have fallen instantly in love with him. He would have been everything she didn't have in her life with Thomas, everything she'd apparently yearned for and maybe hadn't even realized it.

Unlike Mo, her sister wouldn't have seen beyond the veneer and the money and prestige. "I wanted to talk to your father."

He frowned. "Why?"

"To tell him that I knew what was going on at your nonprofit animal shelter and probably all you and your father's other businesses—and so did Tricia."

"What are you talking about?"

Did he really not know? No, Tricia would have told him, wouldn't she? She would have given him a chance to explain.

"I'm talking about the reason the woman you say you loved is dead."

He shook his head, looking confused. "You think it has something to do with the shelter?" He raked a hand through his blond hair. "You can't possibly think that I… I loved her," he said with both conviction and what sounded like pain. "I would have done anything for her. Anything."

"You said that before. What *did* you do for her?" Mo asked as she hugged herself against the night chill and the knowledge that she was taking a chance with her life being here with him. She glanced toward the house. She doubted anyone but Brick knew she was coming out here.

"What are you trying to accuse me of?" he demanded, some of that anger she'd seen before surfacing.

"You said she wouldn't leave Thomas, or was it the baby that was the problem?"

He stared at her as if in disbelief.

"What happened between you and Tricia at the end?"

He shook his head. "I told you. She broke it off."

"And you never saw her again. You never tried to change her mind. You never went by her house."

His gaze narrowed as he settled it on her again. "The nanny saw us, didn't she?" He let out a bitter chuckle. "I thought at least she would have told you or Thomas what she'd overheard, but I guess she was busy with her own…problems."

"I know you were angry, much as you are right now."

He seemed to catch himself and draw back, pulling in his ire as he dropped his voice again. "She did break it off, but then she changed her mind. We were going to raise Joey together. She was going to tell Thomas but then Joey was killed, Natalie was arrested…"

"She never told Thomas."

Jeffrey shook his head. "You know Tricia. She was devastated by all of it, but Thomas was inconsolable. She couldn't do it. She begged me to give her time."

"And when you didn't—"

"Why are you so determined to make me the villain?" he demanded. "I told her she could have all the time she needed. I was a mess, too. I'd been looking forward to us being a family. With Joey gone…" He looked away. "She wasn't sure she wanted to risk having another child. I told her we could adopt. We were planning a future together. Why would I kill her?"

Mo studied him in the faint light coming from the house and realized that he at least believed every word of it. And she believed that he'd loved Tricia as she saw his eyes fill. He hastily wiped at them as the glass doors into the house opened and his father called his name.

"I have to go," he said and cleared his throat. His

watery gaze met hers. "I loved her. If I'd had any idea that she might..." He shook his head, reached for her hand and squeezed it. "I miss her so much."

With that, he walked back toward the house and his waiting father.

Mo stood at the edge of the patio, looking out across the mountaintops into the darkness beyond. Lost in her thoughts, she started when she felt a hand on her arm and spun around to find Brick.

"We need to get out of here."

ON THE WAY off the mountain, Mo told Brick what Elroy had told her.

"Money laundering?" He shook his head. "And your sister knew?"

"Apparently. Why else would she copy the financial records? Tricia was a whiz at math and loved all that stuff, while just the thought makes my head hurt. She either recognized what was going on or at least suspected."

"Your theory is that she told JP?" He heard Mo hesitate.

"She was in love with JP. I believe she found the papers at his father's home outside of Red Lodge. I think she went to the old man."

He shot her a look. "Then he killed her to keep her from coming forward?"

"Also from telling his son. According to the lecture series flyer that Quinn gave me that day, the animal shelter was something he did for his son. If JP knew how it was really being used..."

Brick shook his head. "JP has to know. Whoever came by Tricia's house that day was someone she knew and trusted. Otherwise she wouldn't have opened the door to him." He saw that Mo hadn't wanted to believe it.

She put her face in her hands for a moment. "How could a man who professed his undying love for her kill her?"

"You're a homicide detective. You know. She'd hurt him. He could have lied about this rosy future the two of them had planned. It could be a case of *if I can't have her, neither will Thomas*."

"That isn't love," she said, removing her hands to look over at him.

"No. But love and hate can be two sides of the same coin…"

"I guess I've never been in love."

He considered her for a moment as he drove down from the mountain into Meadow Village. "Never, huh? Maybe we have that in common."

She didn't look at him and asked, "Where are we going?"

He hadn't really known where he was headed. After everything she'd told him, he had to assume that Tricia wasn't the only one who'd suspected something was going on with Jeffrey Palmer's non-profit businesses. The self-made man could be in handcuffs by now—and so could his son. "I hadn't thought—"

"Let's go to your apartment."

"To my apartment?" He must have misheard her.

"Are you sure about that?" She shot him a look. He held up one hand in surrender. "My apartment it is."

He could feel her gaze on him. As he pulled into the parking spot behind his apartment, he asked, "Are you sure about this?"

She chuckled. "It's the only thing I've been sure about for a very long time."

Brick met her gaze in the glow of a streetlamp up the block. "You know my reputation. I don't want to hurt you."

Mo smiled. "You won't because whether you know it or not, you're as crazy about me as I am about you."

He laughed. "You think?"

"I *know*." Her words came out a whisper, as light as a caress.

He studied her in the dim light, realizing that he was a captive to everything about her—and had been since the moment he broke her out of jail. "Are you ever unsure about anything?"

"*Everything*, but this." She leaned toward him, cupping his face in her hands, and kissed him gently on the lips.

He drew her to him, buried his face in her hair and whispered, "Do you know how badly I want you?"

"As much as I want you," she whispered as she leaned her head back to let him trail kisses down her throat. He felt her shudder, his desire spiking, as his kisses reached the rise of her breasts. He could see her hard nipples through her bra and the fabric of her blouse.

"You are so dang sexy. I want to take you right here."

"What's stopping you?" she asked, her voice cracking with emotion.

He chuckled. "Bucket seats," he said and drew back to look into those blue eyes of hers. He took a breath, suddenly terrified. He didn't just want this woman. He *wanted* this woman, all of her, for keeps. He'd never felt like this and it scared the hell out of him.

"You ready to see my apartment?" he asked. "It's not much to look at."

"I doubt we'll be looking at the decor." She reached to open her door.

He caught her before she could get out, and opened his mouth to say what? He'd never know because she put a finger over his lips and shook her head.

A low, seductive chuckle rose from her lips. "We're acting as if this is the scariest thing we'll ever do. It just might be because I suspect there's no coming back from it." With that, she exited the pickup.

Brick sat for just a moment before he opened his door and followed her. He actually fumbled opening the door. He felt tongue-tied and uncertain as if this was his first time. In so many ways, it was.

He held the apartment door open and Mo stepped through. The moment he entered and closed the door behind him, she turned to him and, stepping forward, she began to slowly unbutton his shirt. She looked up at him with those big blue eyes and he was overcome with a longing for something he'd never experienced before. He lowered his mouth to hers and knew he was lost.

Mo lay in Brick's arms. They'd finally made it to the bed. Earlier, the moment the door had closed, they were tearing at each other's clothing. They had been headed here for some time, she knew, but she hadn't expected the kind of passion they'd inspired—and neither had Brick, it seemed from the dazed look on his face.

After their crazed lovemaking, they'd lain on the floor, unable not to laugh as they stared up at the ceiling and tried to catch their breaths. After a few minutes, they looked over at each other. She remembered looking into those deep blue eyes of his and feeling…love and desire, hotter than a Fourth of July firecracker.

They'd made love again, slower this time, but with no less passion.

It was crazy, no doubt about it. They hadn't known each other but for a few days. Mo thought of her sister. Tricia would have said that they didn't know each other, that they needed to take some time, that they didn't even know where this was headed.

But then again, Mo thought, maybe her sister wouldn't have said any of those things. Tricia had fallen in love with a man who wasn't her husband. That she could do something like that given how straight-laced she was… Well, Mo smiled to herself. Maybe Tricia would have understood, maybe even approved since the only two people who could get hurt were Mo and Brick.

Mo started at the pounding on the door. She shot a look at Brick. "Your father?"

He shrugged and got up from the bed to pull on his jeans. She grabbed what she could find of her clothing and hurried into the bathroom and closed the door. She could hear voices. The marshal?

She was dressed pretty much by the time Brick tapped on the door.

"There's someone who needs to see you," he said.

She opened the door and looked out. Her brother-in-law, Thomas, stood just inside the door—which was almost in the middle of the tiny studio apartment.

"Thomas?" she asked, stepping from the bathroom. Out of the corner of her eye, she saw Brick pull on a shirt. They were both barefoot and she hadn't been able to find her bra. Her body still tingled from their lovemaking and she knew her cheeks had to be flushed. "What are you doing here?" she asked, catching the tumble of covers on the unmade bed out of the corner of her eye.

"I have to talk to you," he said, a muscle jumping in his jaw as he looked from her to Brick. "I had a feeling you'd be here." He didn't sound approving, which instantly got her hackles up.

"We should step outside." She moved toward him even as he glanced pointedly at her bare feet. "This won't take long," she said to both him and Brick. Once out on the outdoor second-story landing, she demanded to know what he wanted.

As if seeing her ire, he said, "I'm sorry, but I had to talk to you. I came up after Jeffrey called me, but when I got there, he and JP were being arrested. Do you have any idea what is going on? Does it have something to do with Tricia's death?"

His words stopped her cold. Did he know about Tricia and JP? "Why would you ask that?"

"Because she worked at that animal shelter they owned."

"Remember, I was suspended. I don't know what charges are being brought against them," she said truthfully.

"It's not just that," Thomas said. "I found something in Tricia's closet, hidden in the back."

"Why were you digging in—"

"It's a box with a note on top that says I am to give it to you."

She took a breath and let it out slowly. "Did you look inside?" Of course he would look. Any normal person would.

"There were some papers in a manila envelope. I couldn't make heads or tails out of them."

Mo nodded. "She left some other ones for me, as well. You don't need to worry about it. I'm taking care of it." She started to turn back to the door inside. The night air was chilly. Brick's warm arms called to her. She hadn't let herself admit it, but she felt safe with him. Safe and protected in a way that didn't take away her own strength, her own ability to take care of herself.

"It wasn't just paper," Thomas said. "There was also a key to what appears to be bank security box in the bottom of the envelope. I wasn't able to open the box at the bank, but I thought with your police connection…"

She stopped midstep. A safety deposit key? Maybe Tricia had left something even more important. Mo still wanted a letter or a note from her sister. She knew Thomas did, as well.

"Give it to me and I'll see what I can do," she said, holding out her hand.

"I don't have it. I locked it up in my desk at work until I saw you. I didn't expect to find you here in Big Sky or I would have brought it."

She studied him in the faint starlight. "Why are you here if you hadn't known I was?"

"Jeffrey. He called to say he needed to see me."

"About what?"

"He wouldn't say. I just assumed it had something to do with one of his seminars. He had approached me about working for him if I ever thought about leaving my pharmaceutical job."

This surprised her. "Were you thinking of leaving it to work for him?"

Thomas let out a laugh. "Not now that he's been arrested. Listen, I'll let you get back to…" He waved a hand toward the apartment door. "I'm helping lock up Jeffrey's house after the FBI are finished."

"I didn't realize you and Jeffrey were that close." She could tell the question irritated him.

"It's not just me. There's a group of us who have volunteered to help. I'm sure he'll be out within hours once he calls his lawyer." Mo wasn't so sure about that, but she kept her thoughts to herself. "I plan to drive back to Billings tomorrow afternoon," he was saying. "If you're back by then, why don't you stop by my office?"

"Tomorrow's a Sunday. You normally don't work—"

"I like working on the weekends. It gives me something to keep my mind off everything." He must have seen her hesitation. "Or you can wait until Monday or whenever to get the key. Up to you."

He had to know how anxious she was to find out what Tricia had left for them. "I'll drive over tomorrow. I'll call when I get to town." In the meantime, she wanted to spend the rest of this night with Brick.

BRICK'S CELL PHONE brought him swimming up from the wonder of deep, nightmare-less sleep. For a moment, he couldn't find his phone, he was so wrapped up in Mo's warm body. His hand snaked out. He felt around on the table beside the bed and finally found it by the fourth ring. "Hello?" His voice was rough with sleep and the remnants of a night of lovemaking.

"Brick?"

His mother's voice brought him fully awake. "Mom?" Through a crack in the curtains he could see daylight just breaking behind the mountains. He untangled himself from Mo to sit up. She sat up as well, concern in her expression as she turned on the night-light. "What's wrong?"

"It's your father," his mother's voice broke. "He's had a heart attack. I'm at the hospital with him." The words hit him like thrown stones. "Your uncle Jordan is here with me. We're waiting to hear word on his condition. The rest of the family is on the way."

"Mom, is he..." Brick realized he couldn't say the words. But she wasn't listening. He could hear voices in the background. He felt his heart drop. What was happening? "Mom? Mom?"

"The doctor says they're flying him down to Bozeman to the ICU. I have to go. You can meet us there."

Brick disconnected and looked at Mo.

"I HEARD," MO SAID quickly, squeezing his arm. "Go."

He turned to pull her into a hug for a long moment before he released her and swung his legs over the side of the bed. "Come with me?"

"Brick, I'm the last person your father would want to see—let alone right after a heart attack."

"You know that's not true," he said as he pulled on his jeans and looked around for his boots.

"I'll follow you to the hospital for an update. Then I have to go to Billings. Until I have those papers and that key in my hand..." When she'd come back into the apartment last night, she'd told him everything Thomas had said. He'd insisted that the two of them would go to Billings first thing this morning.

"I know," he said, turning to look at her. "I just don't like you going alone. Even with the Jeffrey Palmers under arrest, they can still get word out to their...associates. You're in danger if they fear the evidence your sister found is more damning than what the feds already have."

She shuddered, well aware of how powerful the men were—and what kind of friends they must have made in the money laundering business. Also, she didn't want Thomas figuring out a way to get into the box without her. She had a bad feeling that she needed to be there when the box was opened.

"Once I have the papers and whatever was in that safety deposit box..."

"I know. Just be careful and call me as soon as you have everything and are safe," he said.

"I will." She climbed out of bed to kiss him, pressing her body against his as if to memorize the feel of him. He groaned and kissed her hard, bunching the fabric of the sheet she had wrapped around her as he held her to him. She didn't want him to let her go and that told her how afraid she was that something would keep them apart. "I'll call you later to find out how your father is," she said.

He gave her another kiss and released her, though with obvious reluctance.

"What are you doing?" she asked as he pulled out his phone and called the marshal's office to inquire about her car. "You don't have to do that."

He smiled at her and mouthed, "Yes I do," as he asked that one of the deputies bring her vehicle to his apartment. "Just leave the keys under the mat. Thanks." He disconnected. "I'm not leaving you high and dry without your car."

"Stop worrying about me and go. I know how anxious you are to get to your father."

Brick nodded as he pulled on his boots. "Be careful and hurry back to me." His voice sounded rough with emotion.

She swallowed the lump in her throat. "I will." She touched the tip of her tongue to her lower lip, remembering their night of shared intimacy as he recovered his shirt.

As he started for the door, he stopped to look back at her as if hating to leave her. She knew the feeling. Being in his arms, she'd felt free of pain, her heart lifting, her blood a welcoming hammer in her veins. She would have given anything to never leave this bed, never leave this man.

What surprised her even more were the tender feelings she felt for Brick. She'd gotten close to him in a matter of days, something completely unheard of for her, especially with a man. Now he didn't want to leave her any more than she wanted him to.

"Don't worry," she quickly assured him. "I can handle this on my own. You just worry about your dad. I'll call later to see how he's doing. Once I have whatever Tricia left, I'll be back. My prayers are with your dad and the rest of your family. Call me if you need me."

His gaze softened in the early-morning light as he opened the door. "I suspect I am always going to need you." He looked as if he wanted to say more.

"Don't worry. We're not done. Whatever it is you want to say to me, there'll be time."

Brick picked up his Stetson. "I forget that you're always right. Hope you are about this."

"I am." And he was gone.

She stared at the closed door until she could no longer hear the sound of his pickup engine. Even then, she didn't want to move. She still felt wrapped in last night's lovemaking. Brick had been a generous, thoughtful lover. He'd made her feel things she'd never felt before. Afterwards, they'd lain in each other's arms, needing no words.

They'd been spooned together when he whispered next to her ear, "You were right. I'm crazy about you."

She'd smiled and reached back to touch his stubbled cheek. "You're going to get tired of saying that." He'd chuckled and pulled her closer and she'd closed her eyes, drifting off into a sleep free of nightmares.

Still warm with the memory, she headed for the shower.

SITTING NEXT TO the hospital bed in ICU, Brick held his father's large, sun-browned hand in his two hands. He studied the scars and brown spots as if all the man's secrets were hidden there. The doctor said Hud was out of the woods. He'd been lucky that it had only been a mild heart attack.

There would have to be some changes, the doctor had said. Less stress, more dietary restrictions. Brick had seen the relieved look on his mother's face, the tears in her eyes at the good news.

"He has to retire," she'd said. "But will that kill him?"

Brick had shaken his head and hugged her. "He

can live vicariously through me, if he lets me back on the force."

"It won't be easy," his mother had said, worry etched on her still pretty face.

"Dad's tough. There isn't anything he can't handle. He'll handle retirement. Maybe there'll be a few grandkids for him to chase around."

She'd smiled. "He would love that and so would I. Thinking of anyone in particular?"

"Angus and Jinx," he'd joked. He would imagine his twin would be all for a passel of kids.

"What about you?" Dana had asked.

"If I found the right woman…"

She'd swatted playfully at him. "You can't fool your mother."

Now he thought about the future for not just his father and mother and the rest of his family. He was worried about Mo and what she would find in that safety deposit box at the bank. He knew how anxious she was to get the key. Maybe, now that his father was out of the woods, he'd drive down to Billings and—

"Brick."

His head jerked up and he looked into his father's eyes.

"You're awake." He let go of his father's hand. "I need to get Mom. She made me promise—"

"Just a moment. I need to say something to you."

"Dad—"

"I'm proud of you."

Brick chuckled. "I know that."

"Do you? Of all my children I've given you the hardest time. It's because you are so much like me and yet also like your mother. What a deadly combination of our free spirits. I realized that I've never told you..." He coughed.

"You really don't have to do this now."

"I do. When I felt that pain in my chest..." His father's eyes filled with tears. "I thought I might not get a chance..." His dad coughed before he added, "I like her."

Brick frowned at him, not sure who he was referring to.

"Mo. She suits you. Don't let her get away."

He laughed and patted his father's hand on the bed. "I don't intend to. But if I don't let Mom know that you're awake she will never forgive me." And yet he didn't want to leave his father. "Thanks, Dad."

His father's eyes closed again. He stepped out into the hall to see his mother headed in his direction. She looked alarmed at first until she saw him smiling. She handed him the cup of coffee she'd brought him and hurried to her husband's side.

Brick thought he'd give them a minute and walked down the hallway away from his dad's room. As he did, his cell phone rang. He stepped into the stairwell to take the call. He'd thought it would be Mo and he really needed to hear her voice.

"Deputy Savage?" The voice was that of an elderly woman. "This is Ruth Anne Hager." The name meant nothing to him at first. The elderly woman had to remind him that he was the one who had approached her.

"I live kitty-corner from the woman who died."

"Oh, yes, Mrs. Hager, I'm sorry."

"It's Miss, but you can call me Ruth Anne."

"All right, Ruth Anne." He waited.

"You said to call if I thought of anything. The other day I was busy with my grandson when you stopped by and didn't have time to even think, let alone recall what happened weeks ago. But since then, I got to thinking. I did see someone go into the back of the house that day. I recall because I was waiting for my trash to be picked up. I'd made some cookies for the men and didn't want to miss them. They're partial to my toffee cookies and they do such a good job, I like to make treats for them."

"You saw someone go into the back of Tricia's house," he gently prodded.

"I was surprised to see the husband return," the woman said. "He never came home at this time of the day, let alone park behind the house. I thought he must be ill."

Brick held his breath for a moment. "You're sure it was her husband?"

"Yes. He was always so punctual on when he came and went. Same time every morning, home same time every night all week long. I liked that about him. Seeing him in the middle of the afternoon on a workday, I was worried."

"What did he do?"

"He went into the house. I'd seen the nanny come

out not thirty minutes before that as if headed for the store. That nice-looking young woman. I can't believe what they are saying on the news."

"How long was her husband inside?"

"Well, the two men who pick up my trash came by. I went out to take them their cookies. They always comment on how nice my backyard looks and how neat I keep the area around my trash containers."

"So you visited for a while. Did you hear any noise coming from the house?"

"Their truck was still running so I wouldn't have heard anything but maybe the other neighbors might have. Did you talk to them?"

He and Mo had. "They didn't hear anything."

"I'm sure everything was all right because I saw him when he left. He did seem a little upset, but he wouldn't have just gone back to work if he'd found her. He wouldn't have left her, now, would he?"

The moment Brick got off the phone, he called Mo. Her cell went straight to voice mail. "I need to talk to you before you see Thomas. It's urgent." He left the message, then thought it more likely she would see a text.

T went home day Tricia died.

He sent it and then hurried into his father's room, where his mother was sitting next to the bed. He quickly told them his suspicions.

"I'm afraid she might not get the message before she sees Thomas," he said.

"Call the Billings police," his father said.

Brick shook his head. "I can't trust them after what happened with me."

"Then go," Hud said and reached for the phone beside the bed. "I'll get you a patrol car so you can use the lights and siren. It will get you there much faster."

MO THOUGHT ABOUT her sister, missing her, as she rode up the elevator to the top floor of the office building. As she stepped out, she had to wipe her tears. Looking around, she caught a glimpse of the Billings skyline through the floor-to-ceiling windows. The rim of rocks the city was famous for gleamed golden in the lights from the city.

She'd never been to Thomas's office. She walked to the wall of glass and tried the door. Then she heard a click and the door opened into a room full of tiny cubicles. Mo realized that she'd never asked Thomas if he enjoyed his work. When he and Tricia had gotten engaged, Thomas had been on his way to medical school. So how had he ended up working for a pharmaceutical company in one of these small cubicles?

The office, she noticed, was empty, most of the overhead lights dark. She started toward the area where there was light when her phone lit up and a notification pinged from her shoulder bag, indicating an incoming text. She started to check it when Thomas called out, "Over here."

She wound her way toward him, thinking of her

sister. Had Tricia been unhappy with her choice in a husband? Had nothing turned out the way she thought? Or had she just fallen in love with JP, something she hadn't seen coming? Something that had turned her life upside down and ended in her death?

Mo still had so many questions and feared she might never get all the answers. But at least the paperwork from the animal shelter had helped bring down Jeffrey and JP. She knew the feds had been building a case for a long time. But after Elroy had taken the papers to the FBI, they had moved quickly.

"Hey," Thomas said as he turned in his chair to look at her.

She took in his cubicle, the small desk, the stacks of paperwork, a few sticky notes on his bulletin board to remind him of meetings. A framed photograph of Tricia sat in the corner. She stared at her sister's smiling face and remembered the day the photo was taken. They'd all been at a family picnic not long after Thomas and Tricia were engaged. Her sister looked happy.

"Are you all right?" Thomas asked, bringing her out of her thoughts.

She nodded distractedly. "Were you happy?"

He blinked. "You mean married to Tricia?" She waited for his reply, not sure why she'd asked. "She was the only woman I ever loved."

"But were you happy?" She motioned to their surroundings.

Thomas looked around as if seeing his office space for the first time.

"I remember when you wanted to be a doctor."

He swallowed and looked away. "Dreams change. We were going to start a family. Medical school would have taken so long and been too expensive and Tricia wanted a home and…" His voice died off. "Why are we talking about this now?"

She knew he was right. She cleared the lump in her throat. "You said you found more papers and a safety deposit box key?"

He nodded and rose. She could see that her earlier questions had upset him. "I need a cigarette."

"I didn't know you smoked."

"I hadn't for years until… It's a terrible habit, but right now I need one. Do you mind?"

She did. The drive had been long. She was tired and wanted to get this over with. Tomorrow her partner had said he would go with her to the bank to get the safety deposit box opened.

"If you could just give me the key and papers…"

"Maureen, can't we just step outside for a few minutes? Please?"

The empty office felt eerie and the last thing she wanted to do was breathe in secondhand smoke. But what was one cigarette? "Sure. But after that, I need to go." She wanted to get back to Brick. Once she got the safety deposit key, she would drive back to be with him and his family.

Thomas was rummaging around on his desk for his pack and lighter. "This will just take a minute. I hardly ever see you anymore. I've missed you." She watched him dig around nervously in the drawer.

Something shiny caught her eye on his desk. A lethal-looking silver letter opener. She tried to make out the design, moving the stack of papers until she could see the logo: MSD, Inc. The name of the corporation that ran the nonprofit animal shelter when Tricia met JP? Her heart bounced in her chest.

"Got it." Thomas said as he pocketed his cigarettes and lighter. "We can go outside."

Mo heard her phone ping with another text. She started to check it when Thomas took her phone out of hand.

"You can do without this for a few minutes. I'd like your undivided attention for once," he said, putting the phone down on his desk next to his computer.

As he turned out of the cubicle, she impulsively picked up the letter opener, tucking it into the back waistband of her jeans and covering it with her shirt and jean jacket.

"Coming?" he asked, looking back at her.

She saw something in his gaze. Suspicion? She was sure he hadn't seen her pick up the letter opener. But he did glance at the desk as if he couldn't remember what was on it. Important papers he hadn't wanted her to see? Or something else?

She felt foolish for taking the letter opener. Did she really think taking it would be any less of a reminder of Tricia's betrayal once her affair with JP came out? And she feared it would come out now that he'd been arrested. Tricia had known something was wrong. Would she have blown the whistle had she lived?

Nor was it necessarily strange that Thomas had the letter opener. Tricia could have picked it up at the animal shelter and given it to him before the affair.

Or maybe he'd gotten it from Jeffrey Palmer Sr. The man probably gave them away at his seminars. Thomas having it didn't mean anything. And yet her heart was pounding like a war drum in her chest. She was so sick of all the secrets and lies and worse, the suspicions. Thomas was making her nervous.

"I just need a quick cigarette," he said as he unlocked a door at the end of the long, dimly lit room. It opened onto a set of stairs that rose to another door. He motioned for her to lead the way.

The stairs were even more dimly lit. Their footfalls echoed as they climbed up to the next door. Thomas opened it.

Mo stepped out onto the dark rooftop, Thomas right behind her, and felt a chill that had nothing to do with the summer night air.

Chapter Eighteen

Mo hesitated on the rooftop. She'd never been that fond of heights.

"Come on, you have to see the city from over here." Thomas moved past her, leading the way to a corner of the roof where there were a couple of benches and a planter. She could smell stale cigarettes and see a can filled with butts.

Thomas lit a cigarette and stepped to the edge. "Quite the view, don't you think?" He took a drag. From where she stood, she could see that his hand was shaking as he put the cigarette to his lips again.

Mo moved closer to look out over the city. The view really was breathtaking. But she felt anxious and more nervous than she wanted to admit.

Thomas exhaled and squinted through the smoke as he looked over at her.

Mo felt a frisson of apprehension move through her. From the look in his eyes, he'd brought her up here for more than a cigarette.

"There's something I've been meaning to ask

you," he said quietly. "How long have you known Tricia was cheating on me?"

She felt as if the air had been knocked out of her. Any doubt she had about whether or not Thomas knew was answered in that heartbeat. There was also an alarming sharp edge to his question, accusation as jagged as a hunting knife's blade.

"I didn't know. Until a few days ago." She met his gaze. "Tricia didn't tell me. I never would have suspected. I didn't believe it at first."

He let out a hoarse laugh. "I know what you mean." His eyes narrowed again. "You and Tricia were always so close. I thought if anyone knew what was going on with her, it would be you." He waited a beat, then added, "So you know about JP."

"I figured it out."

Thomas nodded. "Have you narrowed it down to which one of them killed her? She must have confronted JP and his father and they had to stop her from going to the cops."

It still hurt that her sister hadn't come to her. Mo felt her aching heart break a little more. Tricia hadn't trusted her. Not until it was too late. She pressed her hands to the top of the short parapet wall and stared out at the city, the lights blurring through her tears.

"It had to be someone Tricia trusted, otherwise she wouldn't have let him into her house—let alone accepted a drink from him." Still she didn't look at Thomas.

"A drink?" he asked, sounding confused.

"Her ashes. I took some to the lab. It's amazing how far forensics has come. There was a time when a person could have a body cremated to cover a crime. Not anymore." At least that much was true. "She was drugged." It amazed her sometimes how easily she could lie.

Thomas angrily snuffed out his cigarette and lit another, his hands shaking so violently that it took several tries. "Drugged?"

"How else would the killer have been able to put a noose around her neck without her fighting back?" The image turned her stomach along with the acrid scent of Thomas's cigarette smoke.

"How did you find out about Tricia's affair?" she asked.

He made a guttural sound. "Jeffrey called me."

Mo closed her eyes, imagining the pain Thomas had felt to have the man he idolized be the one to tell him that his wife was having an affair with the man's son. She turned to look at him. "I'm so sorry."

"Tricia and Thomas, the perfect couple, isn't that what everyone said?" His gaze hardened before he broke eye contact to look out over the city. "And after everything we went through, Tricia finally getting pregnant. We were going to be a little family. Only something was wrong with our baby. *Our baby.* What a laugh."

She could hear the pain and anger in his voice, the night growing colder as a breeze moved like a specter across the rooftop.

Thomas let out a stream of smoke and looked over at her. "Guess how I felt when the doctor told me that they wouldn't be needing my blood for my son's first operation because it wasn't a match?" He nodded, smiling a monster's twisted smile. "I knew Joey wasn't mine. What I didn't know was that Tricia was no longer mine, either. Everything I'd believed was a lie."

"I didn't know about Joey," Mo said quietly.

"No one did." He let out a laugh that sounded more like a sob. "I kept it to myself, still hoping that however Joey had come into existence, it wouldn't destroy our lives. Do you have any idea what it is like to carry a burden like that?"

She couldn't imagine the kind of hell he'd gone through learning of Tricia's deception, her betrayal, and said as much. But it was her sister who made her heart ache. She tried not to think of her last minutes on earth, balancing on a chair with a noose around her neck, knowing that her husband was going to kill her.

Mo tried not to glance past Thomas for the exit. She didn't want to estimate about how far she might get before he caught her. She could feel the letter opener digging into the flesh at her back. All her excuses as to why she'd picked it up, she knew it hadn't been impulsive. It had been instinct. She was a born cop. She calculated how many seconds it would take to reach for it under her jacket and shirt, get her fingers around the handle and pull it. Too long.

She told herself that she had a better chance reasoning with Thomas. But when she met her brother-in-law's gaze, all hope of talking him down fled. He planned to end this up here on this roof tonight.

Chapter Nineteen

Brick sped into downtown Billings, the rim rocks around it glowing in the lights from the city. He turned off the lights and siren a few blocks before the building where Thomas worked. He didn't want him to know he was coming. Mo had told him that it was where Thomas had said he had the papers and key locked in his desk drawer. She was meeting him there to pick them up.

He told himself that there was no cause for alarm. That Mo would have gotten the papers and already left. But he'd tried her phone a half-dozen times. Each time it had gone straight to voice mail. Each time, he'd left a more urgent message. Each time, she hadn't called back.

In his gut, he knew. Mo had realized that her brother-in-law was the killer. As he pulled up in front of the building, he saw Mo's car parked on the almost empty street and felt his heart drop. Mo was in there with a killer.

The front door opened onto a small entry. He ran to the elevator and the information sign next to it.

The pharmaceutical company was on the top floor. In the elevator he pushed the button again and again until the doors finally closed and he felt the lift begin to climb.

His heart was pounding. He tried to tell himself that she could take care of herself. If she saw it coming. But the fact that she was still here, that she hadn't called, that she wasn't taking any calls told him she was in trouble.

The elevator finally came to a stop, the door sliding open. Brick rushed off only to find a deserted office full of cubicles behind a wall of glass. He tried the door. Locked. He looked around, frantic to get inside. He could see a light on deep inside but saw no one.

Spying a fire extinguisher at the end of the hall, he pulled his weapon and using the butt end, smashed the cover and lifted the fire extinguisher out. Moving to the glass door into the office, he swung the heavy fire extinguisher and let it go, shielding his eyes as the glass shattered.

He shoved his way through the shattered glass, felt a shard bite into his arm and catch on his long-sleeved shirt. But he ignored the pain as he rushed in toward the only area that was lit.

"Mo!" he called as he ran, his pistol he'd taken from the patrol car drawn. "Mo!" His voice echoed through the emptiness, sounding hollow. He knew before he reached the last set of cubicles that Thomas and Mo weren't here.

But a suit jacket lay over the back of a chair

nearest the exit. Brick stepped to the desk and saw Mo's cell phone sitting beside the computer. She was here and hadn't gone far. Where was Thomas? Brick picked up the scent of cigarette smoke from the jacket and looked toward the exit. A hardcore smoker couldn't go long without one, which meant there was no way he went all the way down to the ground floor every time he took a break.

He ran toward the exit door and shoved it open to a set of stairs that led up. Taking them, he followed the scent of cigarette smoke as if it were a bread crumb trail.

As he burst out the door onto the roof, he didn't see anyone. But he heard the murmur of voices. His instincts had him closing the door quietly behind him as he moved toward the sound, his weapon drawn.

MO NEVER THOUGHT she'd find herself on a rooftop fourteen floors above the city with a killer. What made it more surreal was that she *knew* this man. She'd loved Thomas like a brother.

"I knew you would figure it out if you kept at it long enough," Thomas said, his gaze locked on her. "Tricia used to say that you were like a dog with a bone when you got something into your head. How could I forget that you're a cop, through and through? Her ashes, huh?"

"When did you realize that I knew?" Mo asked as Thomas lit another cigarette, never taking his eyes off her.

"You forget. You and I go way back, Maureen. I

met you even before I met your sister. I know you. What I don't understand is why you would come here alone tonight to meet me, knowing what I'm capable of doing." He started as if it finally hit him. *"You didn't know."*

She felt the fine hairs stand up on the back of her neck. "You're not a killer."

His laugh sounded full of glass shards. "I wouldn't have thought so not all that long ago, but now..." His expression soured. "But maybe you haven't noticed, I've changed."

She shook her head. "You killed Tricia in a fit of passion, I would imagine. Killing me would be in cold blood."

"It's not all that much different, I don't believe. It's about survival. I don't want to go to prison. I want to live."

She knew in that instant. "Quinn."

He smiled, his teeth looking sharp in the glow of the city below them. "You picked up on that right away, didn't you?"

"So you and Quinn—"

"I wasn't having an affair at the same time my wife was, if that's what you're asking. I got to know Quinn after Tricia died—"

Mo felt a stab of anger at how blasé he was about her sister's death. "She didn't *die*. She was *murdered*."

His gaze narrowed. "You want to hear this or not?"

She didn't really want to. Was she that sure that

he wouldn't hurt her? Or that sure that she could take care of herself?

Right now both seemed foolish. Thomas had fallen in love again. He had even more reason to want to be free of the past and that meant being free of his sister-in-law, as well.

"I got to know Quinn. She's sweet."

"You thought Tricia was sweet."

His eyes narrowed dangerously again. "But I never thought of you that way, Maureen."

His words actually hurt. "You're confusing sweet with vulnerable." Mo had forgotten that her sister had been in love with another boy at college before she'd met Thomas. The boy had broken it off. Had she not realized how vulnerable Tricia had been when she'd met Thomas? Had he recognized it, though, and preyed on her?

She'd thought she had such a clear picture of the past, but now it wavered as if for years she'd remembered only what she wanted to. Thomas and Tricia, the not-so-perfect couple.

Even in the beginning, hadn't she seen tiny flaws in their relationship? Red flags that her sister had ignored. She suspected that Thomas had never let Tricia forget that he'd given up medical school for her. Add to that Tricia's problems getting pregnant—until she met JP.

She told herself she could talk him off this roof. Talk them both off. "I was surprised when you had her cremated."

He finished his cigarette, brutally stubbing it

out with the others. "You think she deserved a nice burial?" He snorted. "When I confronted her, she told me that she had planned to tell me. Leave me, is what she meant, but then she realized she was pregnant. Apparently her lover wasn't interested in fatherhood so she broke it off. Or so she said. But often I smelled him on her skin." His eyes swam with tears. "That's right, your precious sister wasn't just an adulteress, she was going to pass off another man's son as mine." He made a swipe at his tears with the back of his sleeve. "It was just one betrayal after another."

She considered her options. He was standing only inches away. If she made any kind of sudden move, he could grab her before she took a step. He was a good foot taller and sixty pounds heavier. He worked out almost every day. She didn't stand a chance against him even with her training.

"If you turn yourself in—"

He laughed. "And go to prison for the rest of my life? I don't think so. Just tell me this. Does your deputy friend know?"

"No," she said quickly. Maybe too quickly because Thomas smiled.

"When I caught you at his apartment, I couldn't believe it was like that between the two of you. I never thought you'd find a man who you felt was your equal."

"Who said I think Brick is?"

Thomas laughed. "Sorry, *sister*, I don't believe you. I know how distraught you've been over your sister's death. But I never expected you to jump off the roof of my office building."

"I'm not jumping, Thomas." She didn't move even when he pulled the pistol from under his shirt behind him and pointed it at her. She wasn't the only one who had a weapon tucked in her waistband, it seemed.

She met his gaze and saw both desperation and determination. One way or another, she was going off the roof of this fourteen-story building.

Brick moved across the dark rooftop. The glow of the city illuminated a portion of the roof at the corner. He spotted the two figures silhouetted against the city lights—the radiance bouncing off the weapon in Thomas's hand. The barrel of the gun was pointed at Mo's chest. She was talking quietly, cajoling, but the figure opposite her was tense and on alert.

Brick worked his way closer, staying to the shadows. The sound of traffic fourteen floors below drowned out his footfalls. He wanted to rush Thomas, but didn't dare. He couldn't take the chance that the man would get a shot off before he tackled him to the rooftop.

He was within a half-dozen yards now. He could see that Thomas's hand holding the gun was shaking. The man was about to do something stupid, but then he'd already done that when he'd killed his wife.

Unfortunately, Brick couldn't get a shot from where he was without jeopardizing Mo's life. He had to get closer because he could feel time was running out.

MO SAW BRICK out of the corner of her eye. She wanted to call to him, to warn him, but as he stealthily approached, she knew he must have seen the gun Thomas was holding on her. She didn't dare look straight at him for fear Thomas would see and turn and fire.

"You don't want to do this."

"No, I don't. But you've given me no choice, Maureen. I begged you to let it go." His voice broke. The gun in his hand wavered just enough to tempt her.

Taking it away from him was dangerous, but he was getting more anxious by the minute. She had to do something. She could still feel the letter opener digging into her back. "We can both walk away from this."

He shook his head. "Even if Tricia hadn't been your sister, you couldn't forget this. It's that cop in you. You just couldn't leave it alone. That damn Natalie had to open her mouth..." He shook his head. "Did she say how she knew that Tricia hadn't killed herself?"

"No. I never got to talk to her before she died. Maybe she was just suspicious."

Thomas made a sound like a wounded animal. "That would be just like her. She was always watching us, couldn't keep her nose out of our business. I hated having her living in our house. I could see how close Tricia was getting to her. I would see them with their heads together. I'd walk into a room and they'd both shut up as if they'd been talking about me. I'm sure they were. I'd failed Tricia over and over. I couldn't even give her a child."

She had to keep him talking. Brick was edging closer. Once he was close enough… "Tricia loved you. That's why she broke off the affair. She wasn't leaving you."

"Is that supposed to make me feel better?" he scoffed. "Do you really think I wanted anything to do with her after she'd been with him? After she'd had *his* baby? That was supposed to be *our* family. *Our family*. Not his."

Mo felt a shock race like fire through her veins. Joey. "Thomas, the baby, you didn't…" She couldn't breathe as she saw the answer in his eyes. "You killed him."

"He was going to die anyway."

She felt bile rise to the back of her throat. She was going to throw up. "You let Natalie take the blame."

"She would have done it if I hadn't. Don't you think I watch the news? She's under investigation for other murders. You know how badly I wanted a family. I gave up my dreams. I gave up everything." His gaze hardened. "Why haven't you tried to get away or take the gun away from me, Mo?"

"And give you an excuse to coldcock me with the gun and throw me over this wall?"

Thomas took a step toward her. She stepped back and he advanced again, this time pinning her in the corner of the rooftop.

She reached back, supporting herself with one

hand, pulling out the letter opener with the other. "Thomas, don't do this."

"You've left me no choice. I begged you…" His voice broke. "Climb up on the ledge, Maureen. I don't want to hit you. Make this easy on yourself."

"On you, you mean."

BRICK SAW THAT time had run out. He was close now. But not close enough. Thomas had Mo trapped in the corner at the edge of the roof.

"Thomas!" he called out, making the man jump and begin to turn. He'd seen Mo reach behind her as if to steady herself on the short wall an instant before he caught the glint of something long and lethal in her hand.

As Thomas saw Brick, he must have also seen Mo's movement out of the corner of his eye. He swung the gun toward her. The weapon in his hand arced in a circle as she ducked the blow aimed at her head.

The gun caught her in the back, doubling her over on the narrow short roof wall. Turning, Thomas got off a couple of wild shots before he grabbed Mo, lifting her to push her over the wall.

Brick charged, watching in horror as she was lifted up. He saw the flash of the object in her hand as she drove the weapon into Thomas's side. He let out a scream of pain. She struck him again as Brick grabbed him from behind and brought him down to the rooftop. But Thomas didn't release Mo, taking her down with him at the edge of the roof.

Belatedly, Brick saw that Thomas hadn't lost his

grip on his gun. The man grabbed Mo and put the barrel against her temple.

"You both should have stayed out of it," Thomas spat and pulled the trigger. As he did, Mo stabbed the man in the throat with what appeared to be a letter opener at the same time Brick fired his own weapon. Thomas's shot was so close, it had to be deafening for Mo. But fortunately, the bullet missed. Brick's, though, had found its mark. Thomas crumpled to the ground next to her.

Brick quickly pulled Mo up into his arms. He held her, refusing to let her go as he called 911.

Chapter Twenty

There was nothing more wonderful than a summer day in the Gallatin Canyon of Montana. Unless of course it was a warm summer night on the Fourth of July with everyone on the Cardwell Ranch gathered to celebrate.

Brick found Mo down by the creek. She'd spent most of the morning in the kitchen with his mother and aunts, preparing the picnic feast they'd had earlier. He'd loved watching Mo with the other people he loved. His mother had taken to her, and his father seemed pleased that Brick hadn't let her get away. It made his heart swell to see how easily she had fit into the Cardwell-Savage clan. The two of them had moved into a larger apartment in Big Sky. Though anxious, Brick had known to give Mo time.

So much had happened, maybe not even the worst of it on that rooftop in Billings. Mo had lost so much. But if the woman was anything, she was resilient. He'd never met anyone stronger or more determined. In the weeks since, everything had come out about Tricia's and Joey's murders. Jeffrey and JP Palmer were still behind bars, both denied bail because they were flight risks. Jeffrey had money stashed all over the world. Passports with new identities had been found for both of them, although JP swore he had no idea what his father had been doing.

Thomas's body had been cremated, his ashes dumped in the Yellowstone River. Brick had stood beside Mo as they watched the last of him wash away. Once the slug from the campground tree was compared to the bullets in Thomas's gun, they'd known who'd taken the potshots at them outside of Red Lodge. Nor had it taken much to find out that Thomas had hired a private investigator to track Mo. He had known that Mo wouldn't stop until she got justice.

Once the dust had settled, Brick had gotten his mental health clearance and gone back to work as a deputy marshal. With his father retiring, there was going to be an opening for marshal. Hud had suggested Mo might be interested. Brick had encouraged her to apply for the position.

"You really wouldn't mind me being your boss?" Mo had asked, sounding surprised.

"Of course not. You have the experience. I think you would make a good marshal. I'd be honored to work with you. Or for you," he added with a grin. "Just so long as when we walked through our apartment door, you remember who is really boss." He'd laughed just in case she hadn't realized he was joking, and she'd stepped to him and kissed him.

"Are you all right?" he asked now as he joined

her. Moonlight played in the water's ripples, the sky overhead a canopy of stars.

Mo nodded and turned to smile at him. "I was just making a wish on that star." She pointed at a bright one sitting just over the top of Lone Peak Mountain.

"I know that star. I've made a few wishes on it myself." He met her gaze. "Your sister?"

"I wish none of that had happened, but I can't change any of it. That wasn't what I wished for."

"No?" he asked, eyeing her more closely. "What did you wish for?"

"If I tell, it won't come true."

He looked at the star and made a wish before he turned to her. "I'm glad I found you down here. There's something I need to tell you."

She turned her face up to him and waited as if not sure what to expect.

"I love you."

Mo laughed. "I gathered that."

"I don't just love you. I've never told a woman that I love her because, as I once told you, if I did, it would be only if I then asked her to marry me."

She smiled. "You were serious about that?"

He pulled her to him. "I've never been more serious about anything. I want to marry you. I want you to be my wife."

MO LOOKED AT this handsome cowboy and felt her heart swell. Tricia used to tease her, saying she was too picky when it came to men, and no wonder she hadn't gotten married. It was true.

But she'd never thought she'd ever meet a man like Brick Savage. She doubted the Lord had made more than one. She laughed in delight as she looked at him, wondering how she could have gotten so lucky.

"I love you, Brick Savage, and I would be honored to be your wife."

He grinned and kissed her as the fireworks show at the ranch began with a boom that exploded over their heads. Twinkling lights showered down to expire before hitting the ground around them. The summer breeze stirred nearby pines as the creek next to them was bathed in moonlight.

For so long, she'd been looking back. But as Brick pulled her close, she looked to the future. She'd already fallen for his family and this amazing ranch life here in the canyon. Cardwell Ranch felt like home.

The other night, she'd found Brick sitting on the porch after dinner with his parents. He'd been playing a song on a harmonica and she hadn't wanted for him to stop. But he must have heard her approach, because he'd finished the song and turned to her.

"I didn't know you played," she'd said, realizing she had so much to learn about this man and how much she was looking forward to it.

"I didn't play for a long time," he'd said. "For a while, I wondered if I ever would again. But then you came along. You filled my heart with music again."

She'd smiled and whispered, "If that's a line to get me into your bed—"

He'd grabbed her and pulled her onto his lap. "If that's all it takes…"

She'd known long before that moment, sitting out there on his family's porch swing, that she was in love with this man.

"Come on," she said now. "Let's go celebrate with your family."

As they headed arm in arm back to the festivities, more fireworks exploded over their heads. Mo felt as if he were leading her out of the darkness. Ahead was a bright future that she couldn't wait to share with the man she loved.

* * * * *

COMING NEXT MONTH FROM

HARLEQUIN

INTRIGUE

Available July 21, 2020

#1941 SETTLING AN OLD SCORE

Longview Ridge Ranch • by Delores Fossen

Texas Ranger Eli Slater and his ex, Ashlyn Darrow, may have a tense relationship due to their past, but after someone makes it look like Eli kidnapped Ashlyn's newly adopted daughter, Eli will do whatever it takes to protect Ashlyn and her child.

#1942 UNRAVELING JANE DOE

Holding the Line • by Carol Ericson

When amnesiac Jane Doe agreed to let Border Patrol agent Rob Valdez help unravel the mystery of her identity, she never expected they'd find ties to a dangerous drug supplier—and an undeniable attraction to each other.

#1943 SOMEONE IS WATCHING

An Echo Lake Novel • by Amanda Stevens

Fifteen years ago, a monster abducted radio host Ellie Brannon and left her for dead. But now, Special Agent Sam Reece is reopening the cold case, as new evidence has come to light. Ellie must work with Sam to uncover the truth...but was the discovery of new details a coincidence?

#1944 IDENTICAL THREAT

Winding Road Redemption • by Tyler Anne Snell

When Riley Stone goes to Desmond Nash's party in her sister's place, she suddenly finds herself in danger. With someone gunning for the twins, Riley turns to the mysterious Desmond. The intrepid cowboy is determined to keep Riley safe...but only together can they survive.

#1945 K-9 PROTECTOR

by Julie Miller

K-9 cop Jedediah Burke has kept his yearning for veterinarian Hazel Cooper in check for years because their friendship is too precious to risk. But when a sadistic stalker's threats against Hazel escalate, protecting her requires staying close.

#1946 APPALACHIAN PERIL

by Debbie Herbert

An unseen enemy has tracked Beth Wynngate to Lavender Mountain, leaving her no choice but to seek Sammy Armstrong's help. They share a fraught history, but the deputy sheriff is her only hope for survival...

YOU CAN FIND MORE INFORMATION ON UPCOMING HARLEQUIN TITLES, FREE EXCERPTS AND MORE AT HARLEQUIN.COM.

HICNM0720

SPECIAL EXCERPT FROM

HARLEQUIN

INTRIGUE

Finding a baby on his doorstep is the last thing Texas Ranger Eli Slater expects in the middle of the night. Until he discovers that his ex, Ashlyn Darrow, is the little girl's mother and the child was just kidnapped from her. Now they have to figure out who's behind this heinous crime while trying very hard to keep their hands off each other...

Keep reading for a sneak peek at Settling an Old Score, *part of Longview Ridge Ranch, from* USA TODAY *bestselling author Delores Fossen.*

"Two cops broke into your house?" He didn't bother to take out the skepticism. "Did they have a warrant? Did they ID themselves?"

Ashlyn shook her head. "They were wearing uniforms, badges and all the gear that cops have. They used a stun gun on me." She rubbed her fingers along the side of her arm, and the trembling got worse. "They took Cora, but I heard them say they were working for you."

Eli's groan was even louder than the one she made. "And you believed them." The look he gave her was as flat as his tone. He didn't spell out to her that she'd been gullible, but he was certain Ashlyn had already picked up on that.

She squeezed her eyes shut a moment. "I panicked. Wasn't thinking straight. As soon as I could move, I jumped in my car and drove straight here."

The drive wouldn't have taken that long since Ashlyn's house was only about ten miles away. She lived on a small ranch on the other side of Longview Ridge that she'd inherited from her grandparents, and she made a living training and boarding horses.

"Did the kidnappers make a ransom demand?" he pressed. "Or did they take anything else from your place?"

"No. They only took Cora. Who brought her here?" Ashlyn asked, her head whipping up. "Was it those cops?"

"Fake cops," Eli automatically corrected. "I didn't see who left her on my porch, but they weren't exactly quiet about it. She was probably out here no more than a minute or two before I went to the door and found her."

He paused, worked through the pieces that she'd just given him and it didn't take him long to come to a conclusion. A bad one. These fake cops hadn't hurt the child, hadn't asked for money or taken anything, but they had let Ashlyn believe they worked for him. There had to be a good reason for that. Well, "good" in their minds, anyway.

"This was some kind of sick game?" she asked.

It was looking that way. A game designed to send her after him.

"They wanted me to kill you?" Ashlyn added a moment later.

Before Eli answered that, he wanted to talk to his brother and get backup so he could take Ashlyn and the baby into Longview Ridge. First to the hospital to confirm they were okay and then to the sheriff's office so he could get an official statement from Ashlyn.

"You really had no part in this?" she pressed.

Eli huffed, not bothering to answer that. He took out his phone to make that call to Kellan, but he stopped when he saw the blur of motion on the other side of Ashlyn's car. He lifted his hand to silence her when Ashlyn started to speak, and he kept looking.

Waiting.

Then, he finally saw it. Or rather he saw them. Two men wearing uniforms, and they had guns aimed right at the house.

SPECIAL EXCERPT FROM

Charlie Farmington has blamed herself for her stepsister's unsolved murder for years. So when Charlie sees her—alive—she turns to the one person she can trust to help her: William "Shep" Shepherd, her first love.

Read on for a sneak preview of Heart of Gold, *the third book in the Montana Justice series by* New York Times *bestselling author B.J. Daniels.*

Chapter One

"Jingle Bells" played loudly from a nearby store and a man jangled a bell looking for donations to his bucket as Charlie let her apartment door close behind her. Snow crystals drifted on the slight breeze, making downtown Bozeman, Montana, sparkle. Pine scented the air as shoppers rushed past, loaded down with bags and packages after snagging early morning deals.

Charlie had just stepped onto the sidewalk, when she saw a woman standing across the street under one of the city's Christmas decorations. Shock froze Charlie to the pavement, and she stared in disbelief. The woman, looking right at her, smiled that all-too-familiar smile—the one that had haunted Charlie's nightmares for years. Even as she told herself it wasn't possible, she felt the bright winter day begin to dim and go black.

Charlie woke lying on the icy sidewalk surrounded by people. She'd never fainted before in her life. But then she'd never seen a dead woman standing across the street from her apartment either.

As she lay there dazed, she realized that she probably wouldn't have even noticed the woman if it hadn't been for her horoscope that morning. It had warned that something bad was going to happen. Not

PHBJDEXP0920

in those exact words. But when she read it, she'd had a premonition she couldn't shake.

Not that she would admit checking her horoscope each morning. It wasn't that she believed it exactly. She just hated the thought of walking into a new day not knowing what to expect.

Earlier this morning she'd actually considered calling her boss and begging off work. She knew it was silly. But she hadn't been able to throw off the strange sense of dread she'd had after reading the prediction.

Unfortunately, she had a design project that was coming due before Christmas. She couldn't afford to miss work. So she'd dressed and left her apartment—against her instincts. If she hadn't been anxiously looking around, worried, she might not have seen the long-dead Lindy Parker standing across the street looking at her. And she wouldn't have dropped in a dead faint.

Becoming aware of the cold, icy sidewalk beneath her, she struggled up with some help from the onlookers. For a while, all sound had been muted. Now she heard the clanging bell again and the Christmas music from a nearby store. She could also feel a pain in her knees; she must have scraped them when she fell.

"Let me help you," an older man said, taking her arm so she could stand on her wobbly legs.

Her gaze shot to the spot where she'd seen Lindy. There was no one there. If there ever had been.

Charlie felt her face flush with embarrassment. Her foolish feeling was accompanied by nausea. She knew rationally that she couldn't have seen Lindy. Yet she couldn't stop quaking. She'd seen someone. Someone who looked enough like the dead woman to give her more than a start.

It didn't help that her rational mind argued against the chance that Lindy's doppelgänger had just happened to be standing across the street from her apartment smiling that evil smile of hers.